The Naked Mafiosa

Gigliola Castania

Published by Gigliola Castania

Publishing partner: Paragon Publishing, Rothersthorpe

© Gigliola Castania 2025

ISBN 978-1-78792-104-7

Book design, layout and production management by Into Print

www.intoprint.net

+44 (0)1604 832149

INTRODUCTION

I was the presumed daughter of a Mafia Godfather; he was an honest shepherd looking for friendship. We found each other on Facebook and so it began my seduction of Luca Oliveri. Our friendship was at times toxic and littered with bad feelings, but it somehow grew. I began to sow the seeds. Although at first Luca thought it was a joke, that someone had conspired to have a laugh at his expense. But slowly with the help of some sultry chat and photos that left little to the imagination I eventually got Luca to accept the truth. My ultimate goal was achieved when we met in Corleone and became lovers. My seduction of him was complete. But it would be tainted with sadness. Once back in the UK, Luca ended our brief relationship. I was left alone to mourn the loss of only the second man in my life I had truly loved. This is our story, told through our Facebook messages.

Dedicated to Rosario Inzirello

10:12

Good morning, Luca, thank you for accepting my friend request. Looking at your photos, are you a shepherd or do you work on a farm? I write books but I am also a blacksmith. I make some wine racks candle sticks, the occasional gate. Is there a blacksmith in Corleone? I must come next July. I would love to see a Sicilian blacksmith in action. If we are still friends, then it would be nice to meet you in person. Although when you know who my father was you might change your mind about being my friend.

 What way to introduce yourself. Booo.
Okay after all we all have our own way of being.
But are you a man or a woman?
How old are you?
And people unfriend you because of the name?
Anyway, can you send me a photo.

 14:01

I am sorry, but when I say the name most people turn me off. I must be honest, I can understand why, the man was a killer, a bastard but he could still have been my father. I live with his guilt every day of my damned life.

 **15.39**

So, X do you want to show me your face.

Woman. My father was Luciano Liggio, my
mother's name was Castania.

*Because I was older, and Luca was only 42, I was worried
I might scare him off. After looking at Luca's other friends,
they were mostly young ladies with amble chests, some in
Sicily, a lot on the Italian mainland. He listed one of his
interests as women, he was dead right he had hundreds of
female friends.*

No, photo, times have changed in 86 when I
came to Corleone to meet with the mayor and other local
dignitaries, I was treated with respect, I personally did not
feel I deserved. People shook my hand, it was madness. I
want to repay that friendship and respect they gave me,
by using royalties from my book, to help the people of
Corleone. It cannot bring back the people killed at his
hands. But I hope to help those who stare poverty in the face
every day.

**Anyway, if I am honest, it doesn't bother me,
that you may be his daughter, it makes me think the fact
that you don't show yourself.**

That's all.

Well, you haven't blocked me yet, so that is a good sign. I know there will be some in Corleone who will not be pleased to see me there, but I cannot be held accountable for his actions, I am not a mafiosa, I have never killed anyone.

It all sounds like bullshit to me, no one has ever talked about him having a daughter!!!!!

Oh, so it is bullshit, that is why I had one of his paintings on my wall. Then I guess at your age you probably know very little about this man. But in 1986, journalists asked me to come to Palermo to meet with Liggio. My book 'Figlia di Corleone' tells the whole sordid story, it will be out soon read it!!!! Do you really think I would want to be associated with such a man for a laugh? So, I fucked a mafioso, maybe that's just bullshit too?

I don't care what you might think, forget it if you think I am a liar. A mafioso is someone who always gives and hopes to receive respect. I know the truth, am I interested in what you think? Er no.

In a moment of madness, I decided the best way to prove I was a woman, was to send a photo with my dressing gown open to partially reveal my breasts.

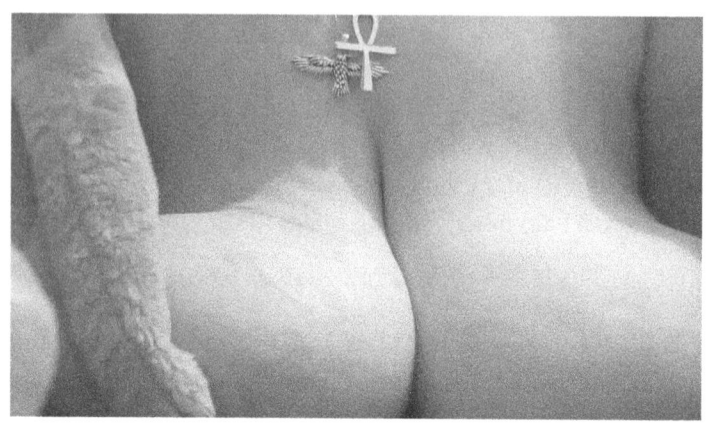

 **19.56.**

You wanted a picture this is the best you are going to get. At least it proves I am a woman, even if I am bullshit. Next July I will find you, then you can call me a liar to my face.

 These are yours?

Then he was a good man.

 Listen a photo with half your breasts outside to convince me.

 20.20.

Oh yes Luca, my big breasts, do you like what you see? The mafioso did, fucked me four times after I shoved these in his face, he adored them.

 **If they are actually yours, I have to congratulate you, you have beautiful breasts.**

But this is not the way to get my trust.

 **22.38.**

Oh, Luca show a man your breasts, and they go all weak at the knees. Thank you for the compliment. They are my best asset, dropped a bit over the years the result of badly fitting bra's. Maybe next July you might get to see Bullshit boobs in person?

26/09/2021.

 **10.57.**

I don't understand shit.

 You made me laugh, saying I was bullshit; I like a man who speaks his mind. At least I laughed at your disrespect, but sweet Luca don't get carried away. Do you think I would let some pathetic shepherd touch my beauties, put his hands between my legs, let alone his cock.

 **11:41**

Then I don't understand dear Gigliola you always talk about the mafia and that you discovered that your father was a mafioso, but don't talk about yourself.

9

12.18.

 What is there not to understand. You disrespect me. Just out of interest Luca do you fuck good, are you passionate? Maybe I might want to find out. Could you bring yourself to fuck some mafia bullshitter, or do I disgust you?

I don't understand what you mean honestly. From what I do understand you are American right. And the fact that you talk like a man.

 Why should I tell you anything about me? I am a fucking bullshitter; Do you not trust anyone? Then I guess as the daughter of a boss of bosses, even if he is now dead, that would make you a little apprehensive. I am a spider in her web, looking out for a fly to ensnare, then I can consume the fly with my passion. I am a highly sexed passionate demanding spider; might you be the fly I am seeking?

15.05.

Oh, sweet Luca, no I am Sicilian, my mother was 17 years old when she was raped by Liggio, maybe she went with him willingly, I never got to ask her before she died. My mother was driven out by her parents. Ended up in the UK, its along story. With breasts like mine do you really think I am a man. Wow are you in for a surprise next July then.

 **I am waiting for you.**

 15.30.

I should be worried when people say things like that, I get nervous, have my breasts turned you Luca, made you into a lusty man? You never did tell me if you are a passionate man? I am very demanding in the bedroom. Am I still a bullshitter Luca shit. Would you share your passion with a person like that? Unmarried, I was once with a Mafioso, but we never married.

 **You don't have to worry, mine is a simple invitation.**
It is not a threat.
But you never married?
So – co-existence.
And then why not.
We can share a bed without any problem.

 16.46.

I have just been chastised by Giovanni, perhaps one in the organization still alive who remains loyal to Liggio. He is 86/87, I think. I call him the oracle; he is like a father figure to me. He is worried that I am senseless when it comes to Sicilian men.

 **So, who is Giovanni did you say?**

In 1986 Giovanni was instructed by Liggio to check me out. Liggio was worried that his life was in danger, that Riina was keen to shut him up for good and take complete control. Giovanni became my friend, and said he was always there if I needed help. He was the last link I had to Liggio.

 **18.19.**
But I don't thrive on social media.
I am a person who prefers real life to a virtual one.

 There you go again with disrespect, having a dig again. Thinking about your kind invitation, maybe I would be wise to pass. After all, would it not be demeaning, that I as the daughter of a mafia boss, should lower my standards to sleep with some common peasant shepherd from Corleone. I just wanted to get you excited, virtual sex Luca, did you play with your cock sweet Luca. I am such a bitch, but it works every time, men are so easy to wind up.

 18.51.
Then it might have been fun having a bit of rough, I could have made crazy passionate love with you. If I decide I want you, then I will have you, no one escapes this spider.

 **Maybe.**

 **19.23.** There is no, maybe Luca, I think you are just playing hard to get, taunting this poor spider. The problem is your in my head, my pussy aches for your cock. This could go on for months, maybe you should unfriend me, make your escape while you can.

 **19.21.**

> **But I don't think about it,**
> **How do they say.**
> **When the going gets tough, the tough get to play.**
> **It is true I speak to the photo of a stranger, but no**
> **problem.**

 **21.22.**
Fantastic Salvatore, he was no actor, he was a sexual Adonis, his touch was magical, he made every nerve in my body sing with pleasure. I loved adored him, mafioso, policeman journalist, secret service, whoever he really was, he was always my sexy Mafioso. Leonardo told me half the women in Palermo wanted to be in his bed. I was the lucky one thanks to my beautiful breasts.

 **21.22.**
> **Because we don't have a chat on video call.**

 But what would be the point we both speak different languages.

 **We can meet without speaking.**

 You just want to see if I am worthy of your time.

Ok
I don't contradict her; she is always a respectable
woman.
Let's kiss the hands of Donna Gigliola.

The next thing I knew Luca had sent a You tube clip of the theme from the Godfather. I felt this was Luca's way of saying he was actually in the family.

 You are Mafioso, you can trust me with Omerta.

Omerta for those not familiar with mafia terms is the code of silence Mafiosi abide by. It's a bit like the English expression. See all and say nothing.

 **Yes, of course I trust you.**

 **21.42.**
So, you are confirming you are an M?

 **What the hell am I supposed to do.**

 That's why you sent the video clip, but how do I know you are not bull shitting me!!!!!

 **21.59.**
As a Sicilian you should know better than to joke about the mafia. So are you one of them or not.

 **And who knows.**

 Ok play your stupid game Luca, I will ask Giovanni to get someone to check you out. Goodnight.

 Goodnight to Giovanni from me too.

 Because things are so vitriolic between us now. Are you going to bail out, because of Liggio?

 I did not know him, so I have no reason.

 I don't care if you knew him or not. I am coming to Corleone to write, to visit my grandfathers and fathers grave, after all if what I was told by my mother is true, I owe my existence to him. We don't have to start our own mafia war, we are friends, maybe one day lovers who knows.

But what mafia war.
However, you know my face.
so, Giovanni will not be able to get the wrong person,
to take a look at.
I'll wait for your video call tomorrow.
At least I can see who I speak too, even if we cannot talk.
That photo on your profile is really bad.

That why you think I am a man, there are no photos of me until the book is published.
Giovanni won't help me, he says I just wanted to create a mafioso to have sex with, to relive what happened in 86.
Maybe that's true, you could be the lucky guy, reap what you sow, you of all people should know that.

27/09/2021.

10.06.
I didn't understand why Giovanni would not help.

10.36.

I wanted Giovanni to check you out, but he refused. He said I had to fix it myself. That I have to make a decision. I cannot sit on the fence as the English say. Do I want to be involved with the organisation or not. Just because one mafioso could not keep it in his trousers, does not mean every Mafioso will fall at my feet, no matter who my father might have been.

 **So, we do the video call.**

Is it right you will do it.

We will share a video call.

 You understand I cannot talk to a photo of an actor forever.

 I understand but I must be careful, there may be some mafiosi who are worried what might be in my book. It will be published soon. Then everyone will see Liggio's secret daughter, I will be on the tv in the media. You say you are a mafioso so why should I trust you of all people with my identity.

 **11.07.**

Except I never said I was a mafioso or not a mafioso.

And then I have to trust an Actors photo when you have
seen my face, know who I am.

 What are we talking about?
I understand you have nothing more to tell me about.
Good luck whoever you are.

 11.59.

I should never have shown you, my boobs. A moment of
madness. Whatever. I will have you Luca if the mood suits.
Maybe our paths will cross. As soon as the book is published,
I will send a photo. Remember Luca the spider in her web,
you are the fly, are you ready to fight.

*Luca totally misunderstood, what I had said so came back
with a random reply.*

 **No, I don't fly.**

 13.21.

Sorry Luca are you still playing hard to get, well we will see
in July. Liggio's daughter always gets what she wants. Just
think about my big breasts in your mouth, you are a man
after all, unless you're like the police inspector and are a
prude. Having sex Luca sharing your body with someone else
is the most natural passionate thing two people can share.

*I translated a small draft of my new book I was working on
'In pursuit of a Sicilian lover'. I hoped sending this would*

show Luca I really was a writer, and not some pathetic internet troll.

 **You sent a copy of your book?**

 14.03.
That is not the Mafia book.

 **Ok**

I sent a chapter.

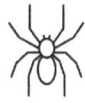 This is an extract from my current book, about how I found out I could be Liggio's daughter. I know you are keen to see me, you will not have long to wait.

 **15.30.**
Yes, but I want to see your face, hear your voice, is that so wrong?

 **17.48.**
I sent that, so you know I am not talking bullshit You can see me in Corleone.

 **Ok I am in Corleone, whenever you want you know how to find me.**

 Thank you.

 **Prego.**

 Dear Luca, I promise you, that as soon as the book is published, I will do a video chat so you can see and hear my voice.

 **As you want.**

 21.27.

Don't take that tone with me, you are the one making such a fuss about seeing me, you are not the only single man in Corleone, I don't really give a shit!!!!!!!!!!!!!!

 **You don't give a shit about me.**

22.23.

Because things were becoming a little strained and it was important for my next book, that he did not disappear from Facebook, as far as I was concerned. I relented and sent a photo taken a couple of years ago at my granddaughters christening.

28/09/2021.

 **10.13**
Is this you?
And why do you decide to send this photo now?

 11.43.

Good morning, so now you have seen me, by the way the baby is not mine.

Yes, this is me. I sent it because you have convinced yourself I am just a bullshitter, and you did not want to talk to a photo of a mafioso. But I need a man not a boy.

 **I am not a boy anymore, even though I am smaller than you.**

 Dear Luca, I meant no disrespect to you, it was a generic comment. But as you can now see I am a mature lady; you are a much younger man. It would be wrong of me to try and seduce you. That does not mean, that next July I might not try. Then you might find me ugly?

 **Well, I have always been attracted to more older women myself.**

 13.32.

Oh, Luca you are making me horny, you're a handsome man.

You have such beautiful eyes; you can see passion in a man's eyes. Could we make beautiful music together. If you don't mind fucking a mafia girl?

 **am not sorry of course I will fuck you, if you want me to.**

 **18.33.**

It doesn't look as if you are attracted to older women by the harem of beautiful young women you have on your face book page. If I don't get a mafioso in Corleone, a bit of you might be worth it. You might just want to rip off my clothes for the hell of it.

 **I don't understand what you mean.**

 When I come to Corleone, I hope to find myself in bed with a Mafioso for the sake of the old days. If that does not happen, might you see me?

19.08.
I am not reserved for anyone let alone you.
Easily make your way with whoever you want.
I only tell you this, I have always been the priority, not the second choice of anyone, much less you Lady Gigliola Liggio.

 You speak almost as if you are a Mafioso. Maybe when I meet Mrs Riina, maybe one of her son's might take a shine to me.

 **21:14**

What makes you think you and I could be lovers?

 Oh Luca, you hurt me. But I love a man with fire in his belly, that confirms to me that you are passionate, I bet you fuck really good, you called me Lady Gigliola Liggio, wow that shows you respect me, more than I gave you credit for. Maybe you and I will become lovers. The only other man I have flashed my boobs at was the mafioso.

But maybe you are right. I am much too good for you, Mr Shepherd, because I should lower my standards. I have a man in Palermo who would love to take me to bed, has wanted to for a lifetime. But he is like my father was, a bastard. I am not that desperate.

 **I have not understood, explain yourself better.**

 **22.00.**

What do I have to explain, you have said you and I will not be lovers Ok. Then you say you are attracted to more mature ladies. Why bother to reply to my messages then. Is this destined to run and run, yes, we will, no we won't!!!!!

 **22:18**

From what you wrote earlier it seems to me, that you have a lover in Palermo, and instead of waiting until next July come to me now.

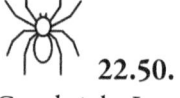 Why would you care, when I come to Corleone? After all I am just plain bullshit, as I have already said there is a mafioso in Palermo, but I would shoot myself first before I would let him anywhere near my body.

 **Understood.**

 **22.50.**
Goodnight Luca.

 **Goodnight signoria Gigliola.**

 Thank you, friend.

 **Prego.**

29/09/2021.

 Good morning, Luca, I owe you an apology, yesterday I showed disrespect to you, I insulted you, I am

24

sorry. You are not, nor never will be second best to anyone. I seem to do a good job of alienating you, when it is not my intention. If I carry on like this I will never get near your bed, let alone share it with you.

15.46
OK
I am not a mafioso, but I can tell you that having a bad temper I have respect for those who respect me, I hate teasing.
be warned I can be everyone's best friend, as well as being their worst enemy should the situation arise.
The choice is yours.
I still haven't worked out if you're serious or joking about this Liggio story.

Oh, my sweet Luca this is not a joke, the complete book tells how I found out just before my mother died, that Liggio could be my father. That my mother was Sicilian, something I had never known. there was evidence at her house, my birth certificate with the name Gigliola Castania on it, Liggio was named as my father, but his name was spelt with an e not an i. Then when he died the mafioso who I thought was my husband said it was all a lie, but the evidence had been compelling, even Liggio himself considered it could well be true.

 **No, I don't know this story.**

Have you not read the excerpt I sent you?

 **No not yet.**

 22.20.

Oh Luca, I am not teasing you, I am the stupid bitch who flashed my breasts to you, to prove I was genuine. no one held a gun to my head, I did it because I want to be your lover. Giovanni knows the truth, about Liggio, he had his ear so to speak. I do have great respect for you, after all you were prepared to give me a chance, and I just threw it back in your face, I have a stupid way of showing you respect once again I have to say I am truly sorry. Gigliola.

 **22.40**

So, we are good Luca? I am not playing, this is not a game, I really like you as a person, would like to know You as a friend, goodnight my dearest Luca.

Dear Luca, I'm such a fool. I have tried to apologise, but it seems you are not in a forgiving mood. I really am sorry; can we not start over? Forget all the mafia talk. Tell me about the farm. The sheep.

 **Until yesterday it seemed I talked to a mafia boss, today you've seemed more like an ordinary person. Goodnight.**

30/09/2021.

 **11.07.**

So, you thought I was a mafia boss. when you really thought I was a man, you call me an ordinary person!!!!!! oh Mr Oliveri, I am no ordinary person I am a mafia Princess, the daughter of a boss of bosses. the Godfather who made the Corleone branch of the Sicilian mafia the all-powerful force that it was to become. You would do well to remember that. I will look out for you in Corleone, only so I can slap your arrogant face. Goodbye Luca Oliveri.

17.17.

I look forward to seeing you lady Liggio.

Why did you write under my photo?
It will be read by everyone you know this right.
my Facebook page is public, and everyone can read.
Erase what you wrote,
this is not the way friends behave towards each other.

I was wrong to do that, but my mafia side came out you refused me. I wanted revenge.

I'm surprised that you are not really mad. I should not have done that, but why should I be your dirty little secret, are you ashamed that people would know about our friendship? You can always block me then you will be free. No need to worry what I might say next.

I have no record of what it was I wrote, because I did erase what I had written. But I'm sure it was not detrimental to his integrity I had just wanted him to respond, after he had been ignoring me all day. I was somewhat confused he had demanded I take down what I had said, now he was asking me why I had removed my post? Sometimes I did get the impression I was talking to two different people it was bizarre. I just sent a thumbs up and waited for a reply. He said goodnight, I replied and that was it.

OCTOBER
01/10/2021

09:57.

Good morning, Luca, I'm sure you have been working for hours. It is not an easy life being a farmer. The landscape looks gorgeous from your photos what a beautiful place to work. I do hope I can visit the farm I am coming in April now when it is not so hot.

Good morning.

Thank you, Luca.

28

 **10:30**
You're welcome.

 **19:21**

If you could ever get over your anger, I'm sure you would give yourself to me, not being arrogant on my part, but just from the way you have spoken, before we fell out. It did seem like it was a distinct possibility. But at the end of the day, you are the one who holds the key, I hope you will open the door and that it will be the first of many times, I do hope so, are you romantic Luca?

 21:16

Goodnight Luca.

 **21:25**

I know I have said goodnight already. Your farm, I wondered is it mixed arable and livestock? Do you have only sheep or do you also have horses and cattle.

02/10/2021

Good morning.

11:50
Good morning.

29

 I'm just asking about your farm, because I'm trying to be an ordinary person. I am not trying to take control of it oh by the way, I'm not going to slap you. Gigliola being childish.

 **13:17.**

At least decide what type you want to be.

 **15:03**

I really don't understand, I can't help who my dad was, so I will be the mafia bitch then. I'm only trying to be friendly forget it. You and your beautiful brown eyes have always been my undoing.

 **That is?**

 What's with the two words, you're so maddening. Block me if you don't want the conversation, oh but that's it, you want me to dangle. the stupid mafia bitch who you got to flash her breasts. who wants to fuck you, wild sex that at least you will understand. Just be grateful I am not like Luciano. Otherwise, when I come to Corleone, I would not be just giving you a slap.

 **Let me see your breasts.**

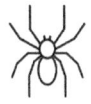 Because?

 **To see how beautiful, they are.**

 No Luca, you are trying to flatter me.

 **So, you can show them to me or not?**
Why not all naked?

Luca are you saying you want to see me naked? Oh no no, this mafiosa only gets naked just before making crazy passionate love. I flashed my breast to prove I was a woman and to get you interested in me.

 **Yes.**

 21:28

Oh Luca, I might be a shitty mafia bitch, but I am not stupid flashing my breasts is one thing. Completely naked are you crazy? So, you can tell all your friends that Liggio's daughter is a slut a whore. No no, Luca. the only way you will see me naked is if we sleep together.

 **But in fact, my friends don't know I am talking to you.**
I know how to keep secrets.
I don't advertise.

 Good for you, there is no way you see me naked. I am not a Peep Show for your enjoyment.

Luca gave what would become his customary trademark, when he was not sure how to reply, an emoji shrug of the shoulders.

 **22:17**

Oh Luca, those brown eyes are calling me. But you don't want to see me naked! All of Me is big, from the head to the bottom, Covid was not good to me. Before lockdown I could cycle up to 10 miles a day , just think how good it will be, when you can undress me in person, touch kiss and caress my breasts with your mouth, before making crazy passionate love with me goodnight. Gigliola.

 **Goodnight.**

 Thank you, Luca.

 **So, you and I will be lovers?**

Would you sell your soul to the devil Luca?

 **No.**

 So, we are not going to be lovers, because I am the closest thing to the devil being a mafiosa!!!

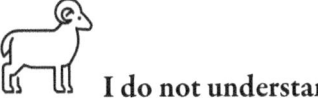 **So, it all ends like this?**
You said you would take me to heaven.

 I don't understand your cold, towards me, now suddenly you decide you might want to sleep with me. You know who I am, okay I am not a practising mafiosa, but Liggio was my father. Do you have a woman in your life? My God you're not a virgin are you.

 **I do not understand.**

 You must know if you are a virgin or not what is there not to understand. Let's see what happens next April when I come to Corleone. You may not find me attractive enough to want to rip my clothes off.

03/10/2021.

 **10:39.**

What Luca is with the emoji. are you a man of few words?

 **Yes.**

 **10:58**

I dreamed of you last night, it means you are mine.

 **12:13**

And what did you dream of?

Can't you guess? I see you in a bar in Corleone, I have a drink and walk out. You follow me, you take off your shades, I see your Gorgeous brown eyes and I am captivated by them. we go to my apartment where you are welcomed, and we Make Love like neither of us has ever done before. All night Luca, repeatedly. but alas it was just a dream. I will

34

get worried if I have another one.

 **It was a good dream.**

 Oh Luca, it was fantastic, So vivid so much passion. I have lived without sex for 26 years. I think that's the problem, 26 years of frustration, I feel like Etna about to erupt.

Really?

Yes, the last man to Make Love to me was a mafioso in 1986. We met again by chance in 1994, when I went to visit my father's grave, he had one of the cemetery staff watching the grave. I could not believe it when I turned around and he was standing there. I loved him, he asked me to marry him, but I was sure he was a mafioso. So, I walked away, but I never stopped loving him. And became celibate, could not bear the thought of another man touching me after the passion I had shared with him. But I realised during lockdown that life was moving on, and it was time to let go. Life is short the days the months the years pass, I decided I wanted to be a woman again while I still have the chance to feel passion the touch of a man on my body.

So, who will be the lucky man?

 **13:11**

Well at the moment I keep dreaming about you. you are in pole position, the problem is, would you like to touch me let alone fuck me.

 **But if you don't even show up, how do I know if I want to touch you?**

 **14:05**

Luca I will be there. I may have a book tour of the island. You asked me if we would become lovers, now you are playing me, it's your right, I am in Palermo for four days. maybe I might see Leonardo, and after all this time he may get to take me to bed, he can dream, I doubt that bridge will be crossed.

 I do not understand.

 You don't need to forget Leonardo he has the morals of a rabbit. a different woman every day. when I come to Corleone, let's meet as friends for a drink, then let's see if there is a spark between us. I find it hard to comprehend that I've gone 26 years without a man inside of me, when I am so highly sexed, but Valerio meant so much to me, the first man I've ever truly loved. I hope he found true love married and had a big family. that life was good to him.

 **I do not understand.**

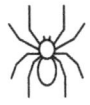 **15:18**

What is not to understand. I come to Corleone, we have a beer or a coffee. We chat as best we can, you then decide if you want to be my lover for two weeks, or even just a one-night stand as the English say. So, what is there not to understand.

 **Come quickly then.**

 16:34

Why, why do you want me to come quickly?

 **So, I see you.**

 17:08

To see if I could be your lover, and you could be mine. at my age I need an experienced lover.

 **17:27**

I always manage to insult you, you might be able to teach me something new and exciting, unbridled passion, how wonderful would that be.

18:13

It will be very difficult to try to maintain a conversation with you, but people who are sexually attracted to each other, do not have time to talk when they are making love. They are usually too busy with their mouths doing other things, like oral sex, oh Luca Oliveri!!!!!!

In the meantime, you could show yourself naked, so I can get an idea what will happen when we meet.

Forget it Luca, I have said no before, and I mean it no, get over it and don't message again if you insist on this course of action.

You with that damned emoji, you will never see me naked unless we are about to get into bed together. Showing my breasts is one thing, but naked no no no. the mafiosa in me is getting mad. I will not sleep with you; I will stick to my own kind. maybe I will get a Sicilian cock in Palermo. Forget you ever talked to me, understand that Luca Oliveri.

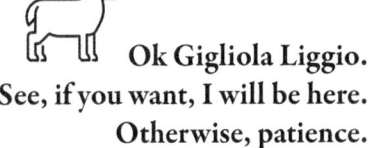 **Ok Gigliola Liggio.
See, if you want, I will be here.
Otherwise, patience.**

 19:22

Yes, I know where to find you Luca Oliveri. Who knows maybe tonight I will still dream about you. Those beautiful brown eyes. I'm not used to people saying no to me. But you have character, however you will not bully me. I have great respect for you, with that good evening. Gigliola.

 **You fell in love with my eyes.**

 Dearest Luca, I am not in love with your eyes, I'm just captivated by them. You can see the soul of a man through his eyes. You look like a kind honest sincere man, a loner I would say, who prefers the company of your sheep over humans, nothing wrong with that I am the same, I have my Ravens, they are my friends, my companions true to me. As I would say your lovely dog is to you, but I am sure we will be good friends, and also lovers.

 **And who knows.**

 **21:39**

Goodnight, Luca.
04/10/20 21.

 Good morning, Luca, another busy day on the farm. I hope the weather is good in Corleone. I dreamed of you again last night. This is becoming a habit, but I have to say a pleasurable habit all the same, here's hoping you have a good day.

 **And what did you dream about this time?**

 **09:11**
Oh Luca, can't you guess, we made passionate love, you caress my breasts, with the hands of a sexy shepherd, then we kissed and caressed with unbridled passion, you were strong and beautiful, but alas it was only a dream.

 **Pity but true.**

 Really Luca, but someone who wants to see me naked, the only thing you can say is pity, but true. Enjoy looking at yourself in the mirror darling.

 **Of course, I say true.**

10:23
Thanks X darling.

11:02
Luca you called me darling, wow are we going to the next level?

You called me darling.

So, I did, slip of the tongue.

Where did the tongue slip?

Sorry, English expression English is my first language after all, I am just learning Italian so that is why some of the words might not make sense. But you don't have to speak a certain language to Make Love, sex has no linguistic barriers. You want to see me naked, how about I see you naked Luca Oliveri?

Be seen naked?

Yes, you wanted to see me naked. So, why can't I see you, then I can swoon over your beautiful Sicilian cock.

41

After all I have been dreaming about it maybe it's time, I see it for real.

 But then would you expect me to do the sam.

 **Of course.
You'll have to start showing up.**

I wondered if this was all game playing on his part. He said I could see him naked, but then implied I had to be seen naked first. How did I know he would not only opt out of the agreement if he saw me naked first, so I called him out on it.

 **15:43**

How did I know you were going to say that. Oh well it is beautiful in my dreams. Seeing it in reality could be a disappointment, the penis is a penis, whoever's slides between your legs. Only that Mafioso he was something else, I knew he was there.

 Luca are you still a virgin, I've asked you this before, but you never gave an answer.

 **I have not been a virgin for a lifetime now.**

 I'm Happy to hear that you may be able to teach

42

me some new things if we get to that point. I think you need to let me into your bed so that I can open your eyes to the true wonders of sexual pleasure.

05/ 10/ 2021

 **07:15**

Good morning sexy shepherd.

 **What did you dream about last night?**

 Sorry Luca, last night I was back in the sea in Cefalu with Valerio the mafioso from 86.

 **You were in Cefalu, are you in Sicily now?**

 **11:11**

No, I am not in Sicily now, that was back in 1986. Then Valerio was one of my father's men who shadowed me. We ended up spending the night together. We started in the sea, then we made love in the shower, then twice in the bedroom. Then he just left while I was sleeping, left a note on the pillow, I was devastated.

 **And why?**

 **11:55**

I don't understand why he went and just left a note.

 I don't understand either, why he just left a note. After we had spent such a terrific night together, he did say it had been wonderful, and that I would be in his mind for days. But to sneak off like that it made it seem cheap and sordid. later on, I found out the real reason, he was falling in love with me. he told me just before I left Sicily, he had to go that night, because if he had stayed, he would never have wanted to leave me. but it was not possible for us to have a relationship for obvious reasons. It was always going to be doomed.

 **Booo.**

 He was older than me, I feel so embarrassed.

 **Why are you embarrassed?**

 12:32

We had met earlier in the week, in my hotel room. Early that evening we had exchanged a glance, it was pretty obvious, that we were both sexually attracted to each other, he just turned up later that night. It got quite steamy, then he just switched off, I think he was worried about my father finding out. I stripped to my panties to try to get him to stay to take me to bed, but he never gave in, even though he did kiss and fondle my breasts. In the end he just man handled me out of the way and went. After I was raped, I disappeared ran away to Cefalu, he came looking for me.

 **Right.**

12:33

You haven't even shown me your boobs today.

I'm sorry I don't understand.

I haven't seen your boobs; I want to see them.

But Luca, you know what they look like it's not as if you haven't seen them at all. you're like Valerio fascinated by them. would you like them in your face, your tongue licking my nipples? your mouth kissing them, anyway, haven't you got a field you'll need to plough.

Come on show, let me see them, your beautiful breasts.

45

 I embarrassed you, oh Luca don't you want to kiss and caress them, I am very disappointed.

 **I do not understand**.

 Well, if we are going to be lovers, don't you want to kiss them? Just go straight to fucking no foreplay, no oral sex? there is no passion if you don't have the foreplay to put you in the right mood.

 **Of course.**
You have to do the foreplay, fingers first in a beautiful wet pussy, then oral sex, you are sucking my cock, so I come in your mouth, then we have wild uncontrollable sex.

 Oh Luca.

 **14:39**
I do not understand.

 **15:32**

Well with all that talk of oral sex then wild sex it has made me want to get you into bed even more now, I have come over all faint.

It would seem all the ladies that have been in your bed will

46

not have been disappointed.

 **It seems not.**

 Oh, very competent, but would I leave satisfied? I am very demanding. I can't get the thought of oral sex out of my head at the moment Oh Luca, I cannot concentrate on my writing.

 You like best to do, or receive it?

 Receive it.

 Why not do it?

 I like to kiss a penis, lick a Man's balls, but not suck it for too long.

 I really like that women suck me off, while I lick them and put my fingers in her pussy at the same time.

 I like being kissed between my legs; I love being

finger fucked. I get really excited and wet, especially if I'm on my knees, in the sheep position, fingers really get me turned on.

 **Even in the arse?**

 Oh no never that. We will never be lovers then, no one sticks their finger or their penis up my bum. I would sooner die before I'd let anyone do that. not even you Luca Oliveri, no matter how crazy about you I am.

 **See you later.**

I must say I'm very disappointed in you, gay men lesbians do it. If you are heterosexual fingers and penises go in your vagina. I really liked you until you said this. Before all I could think about was you kissing between my legs, your fingers inside me making me orgasm, now you have ruined it for me Luca.

Because?
If you don't like it, forget it.

Forget about possible sex with you, or just forget about that?

 **Anal sex.
what are you doing?**

 Oh Luca, are you saying I could have your tongue with your fingers in my vagina. Oh, I just wet my panties at the thought of it, I could suck your cock, but no no anal sex. God, I bet you fuck good.

 **Did you say you wet your panties?**

 Yes

 Wow.

 Yes, wow Luca.

 **Did you put your fingers in it?**

17:34
No, I don't care to play with myself. That's why you have a man to play with you, I was just thinking about your fingers in there. I do not need to worry about dryness with all the vaginal juices that gush out, do you have long fingers?

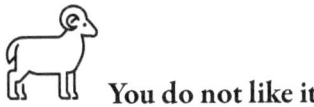 **You do not like it?**

49

17:52

I know men play with themselves; you might as well do it now. It has never excited me masturbating, some women do it, use sex toys. Not me I want a real man to play with me.

 **I don't know who this Valerio is.
And you haven't had sex since 1994?**

I started to realise, that Luca did not always retain information. Again, he was asking who Valerio was, and how long it was since I had slept with a man. Something we had previously discussed, but I was happy to refresh his memory for him.

 The last time I had sex was in 1994, I visited Corleone the year after my father died. I started over with Valerio. we Made Love all afternoon it was like an eruption of Etna, as we embraced in a sea of passion.

 18:39

It is hard to believe when I look like a sex maniac, but I loved him with all my heart, the trouble was the mafia always got in the way. long distance romances tend to breakdown. but I loved him, I could not betray him so became celibate. he had been my world, I wanted to remain loyal to him.

 **Then you will be tight, as if you never had sex.**

 **20:36**

Does that turn you on Luca? Imagine as it tightens around your penis, so I would feel it throbbing inside of me. There's just another problem to overcome you have a hairy chest, that's usually a turn off for me. I like a smooth chest so I can run my tongue down it as it meanders towards your penis.

 **I am sorry, I can't help that.**

 Not half as sorry as I am. would you take me to bed? Must I make do with it in my dreams.

 what makes you think I would have taken you to bed anyway?

 I don't understand you. You were the one that told me to hurry up and come, why if you weren't going to take me to bed would you say that?

51

 **You wrote to me, to start with. You were the one that said you wouldn't take me to bed, because I'm just a shepherd, a peasant from Corleone, and you're a mafia Princess, I forgot a godfather's daughter. I ask you what makes you think I would have!!!!!!**
You lie about only loving this mafioso Valerio!!! did you not write on Facebook that you loved a police inspector?????

21:40

No no Luca, Gianni and I were not lovers, just friends only on Facebook. Papa must have been turning in his grave, me with mafia association being friends with a policeman. It was quite bizarre, Gianni said it was an honour to know Liggio's daughter, I admit I was infatuated with him, but he was very vain, he only loved himself really. He just led me on, he was originally from Palermo but worked in northern Italy, who knows maybe he was a bent policeman, and that's why he was so accepting of me. He was always going on like you about wanting to see a picture of me. I eventually gave in, and he suddenly turned nasty, told me to crawl back into the gutter from whence I had come. I took it very badly and became quite depressed.

 **Maaa.**

 **22:14**

When I come to Corleone will you make crazy passionate love to me?

 **But I have hair on my chest and shoulders, you said that turned you off, now it's my turn to say to you, you should make up your mind.**

 OK that's no then.
You don't want to take a Godfather's daughter to bed, and try to fuck her arse?

 **And why not, sorry.**

 **22:57**

I will go to bed and dream you are playing with me.
Goodnight Luca.

 Goodnight.
If you show me your boobs, maybe I too would dream of playing with you.

06/ 10/2021

 **10:25**

You're a dark horse and looking like a womaniser. Well, the

Godfather's daughter just walked away from you.

 **19:25.**

When I get to Corleone better give this bitch A wide berth,
or my mafia side might be tempted to blow your brains
out. Have a good laugh at my expense, you and your mates.
respect Luca, something it seems you know nothing about.

 **I have not understood.**

 **20:41.**

Remember I have seen your harem. Boy there was I thinking
you were stuck in the mountains alone. When every day
you're having intimate conversations with so many women. Is
that why you spend so much time online, when you should
be looking after my sheep?

 **But do you observe what I do?**

 Jealousy is a dangerous thing, but why should I
worry, when really, I have my eyes on the local Don. It would
be a laugh if it turned out to be you with a big cigar like my
dad smoked.

 **Yes, sometimes I like to smoke a cigar, but not**

because I am a Don. Simply because I like it.

Good job you're not the local don after I said I'd blow your brains out. are there many women flashing their tits at you? You dream of playing with their breasts but not mine, are they not good enough for you.

 **Ok.**

Before you go, your friends with Antonio Riina, is he related to Toto Riina?

Write in Italian I do not understand, you had sex with Toto Riina.

Sorry for the English translation, no I did not have sex with him I was just wondering if Antonio was a relative/nephew, I saw him on the I love Sicily page. If it is it could mean you are a mafioso because your friends with him.

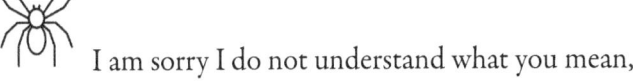

I understand, no Antonio is not the son of Toto. and anyway, I don't like being controlled, let me be clear.

I am sorry I do not understand what you mean,

I am not checking you out I was looking through possible Facebook friends always looking for friends in Corleone your name came up as a mutual friend. Oh, Luca are we having our first real fallout? When we seem to have become so close.

 **The kiss what does it mean?**

 Well, I did say I would blow your brains out. Just a gesture of goodwill. Want to see my breasts again?

 **Yes.**

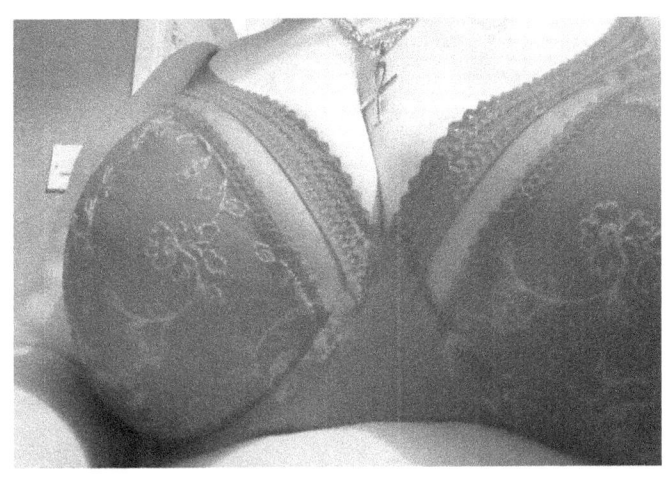

 Goodnight Luca.

 **Goodnight darling**.

07/ 10/2021

 **11:20**
Good morning, lady Gigliola.

18:33.
Good evening, did you think I was ignoring you because you called me darling last night. It was a pleasant surprise but no I've been busy proofs to read, check that the manuscript was edited correctly. So, did you dream of me last night? Tell me what it was like what did you do to me.

 **19:01**
It was a beautiful dream.

 You liked me then, but alas it was just a dream.

 **And yes.**

08/ 10/ 20 21

 **07:37**
Good morning.

 09:46
Good morning, Luca.

 **Welcome back.**

 Thank you.

 **You're welcome**.

 11:56

I'm sorry for that, I had to take a phone call. So, you missed me talking about sex with you, I am too worried to dream of anything over than that bastard of a father, who seems to be taking up most of my time at the moment. I need a good distraction. Do you have horses? I love to ride them as well as men. Oh, how rude.

 **Yes.**

 Oh Luca.

 **16:33**

Sorry Luca, I don't know if I'm coming or going. I am suddenly back on the other side. I have become almost frozen again, loyalty to the mafioso of 86. How long should someone give a shit. it could be you fucking me. Then you could already have a girlfriend, even be married. Although your Facebook page says you're single, I know you don't mess with Sicilian women; do I have to search for another man, but I need you!!!

 **I do not understand.**

As I said previously, after losing the mafioso, I have always stayed away from sex. Then I woke up one morning and realised I missed a man's touch; but if I took a lover, he had to be Sicilian. But I feel shame and guilt, I'm betraying my love for him, which is a shame because I enjoyed our sexy chats.

 **So, you don't want to talk anymore?**

17:23

Luca please. I'm not using you; you are the first person that has seen my breasts in 26 years. Please don't sulk, I am talking intimate with you no one else and I want to carry on doing that.

 **17:23**
I don't understand.

 I am now coming to Corleone in November.

 **And I see you right?**

Luca, there is no one else only you, I come to see you, and only you.
09/ 10/ 2021

 **18:01**
Why don't you show me your nipples.

 **21:55**

Excuse me, you forget who I am. You should show more respect Luca Oliveri. You cannot go making such requests, so we will not meet in Corleone. Gigliola Castania Liggio.

 **OK.**
It is right to clarify things.
Good life Gigliola Liggio.

.

 Thanks, I am sure our paths will cross.

 I really don't think so.

 It doesn't matter, you were probably too inexperienced for me anyway. I wonder how long it will be before I change your mind again.

 Usually, I do not change my mind, the decision remains that.
It is impossible for me to think about it when I make a decision.
Good luck.

10/ 10 2021

 **11:08**

Thank you, Luca.

 I intend to text all day, hope the weather is fine on the farm today? I wish you would change your profile picture you talk about mine I hate the current one of you; it makes you look almost sinister, hiding away those beautiful brown eyes. I know I walked away when you talked about anal sex. You would not force me to do that, if we met would you Luca?

 **16:36**

So how is my favourite shepherd today. This will make you laugh my flight has been cancelled the whole month of November so I will not be in Corleone until December.

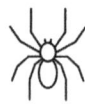 **18:38**

Oh Luca, Luca you are the magnet, and I am a piece of metal which is constantly drawn towards you.

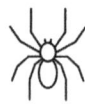 **22:39**

Goodnight Luca.

12/ 10/ 2021

 22:39

So, what kind of day has my favourite shepherd had today? I do hope when I come, we can get together for a drink, even if it's only a coffee, who knows what might happen I am still captivated by those beautiful brown eyes of yours, I so want to see them in reality.

It started to seem as if Luca had meant what he had said, about not changing his mind. There was no reply from any of my messages, I decided to keep the pressure up I would carry on messaging him sooner or later I was hoping the lure of my breasts would be too much for him to resist, and he would miss not seeing them.

13/ 10/ 2021

08:53
Good morning, Luca.

Have I lost my sexy shepherd?
If I must be a hypocrite, I will show you, my nipples. If you will talk to me? I miss you my sexy shepherd.

 18:19

Oh Luca, have you really washed your hands of me? I know I'm a Moody cow, but I still dream of you. I will look for you when I come to Corleone, and we will make beautiful music together, I so hope.

 19:06

So, even the lure of my nipples, Will not get you to change your mind? Think about it, your mouth caressing these beauties, kissing licking them. Not so long ago you so adored them, was upset if I didn't show you them. You said how beautiful they were, was that not true.

I SENT A PHOTO OF MY BREASTS JUST TO REMIND HIM WHAT HE WOULD BE MISSING HOPING IT WOULD STIR SOMETHING WITHIN HIM ONCE MORE.

 **22:48**

Oh Luca, guess I should give up then you're done with me. I've pissed you off so many times. goodbye Luca.

 **OK.**

14/ 10/ 2021

 11:03

Oh, Luca I have to say goodbye for you to answer with an OK!!!!!!!! I want to Make Love with you so much. why do you not believe that.

You have got me Luca; you have such power over me I hope you will change your mind and give in.

I was furious with him; he'd been loving all this attention; I knew this because he always marked the messages which proved he had read them. now he realised, that I really might be going, he decided to respond.

 What power are you talking about?

 Oh Luca, you answered me. The power of frustration it makes me so sad, because you have washed your hands of me also, but I want you so much, I am so sexually attracted to you.

 **12:24**
I see how much I drive you crazy.

 The power Luca, the power you see you have over me it will be like Etna erupting.

I do not believe it.

 Believe Luca, believe it will be beautiful.

 **Yes, like the dream.**

 Oh Luca, I have thought if nothing else all afternoon, other than the thrill of feeling your hands on my naked body. I would like to Make Love to you on a large sheepskin rug. I want to experience your passion, look into those beautiful eyes and take you to my paradise, where we will both swim in a sea of sexual desire. Oh, Luca you don't give a damn about me, I am just massaging your oversized ego.

 **21:29**
Do I have a chance or am I destined to only dream about you?

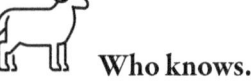 **Who knows.**

 Such power you have over me. I have been kidding myself, I never had a chance with you, my own fault.

Then I got one of Luca's random replies.

 **You're wrong, I do not make fun of anyone.**

 I'm sorry? I didn't mean you were making fun of me; you just didn't say yes or no, so I'm not sure where I stand?

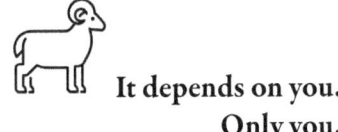 **It depends on you.**
Only you.

I wondered what he meant by this; I had a feeling he was going to ask for more naked photographs.

 For me I imagine we will make beautiful music together. G.

22:53.
Goodnight lover.

15/ 10/ 2021.

 **06:59**

Since you called me lover, take out your nipples.

13:34
I see you don't write anymore.

 17:26

I've been busy did you miss me? What is the charm of my nipples, do you really want to see them? But they could be anyone's. This is the only way to prove I am a woman, woman who wants to fuck with you.

 **Of course, I want to see them.**

 17:57

See Luca it's not that easy to photograph my nipples, you have seen how big my breasts are, and anyway why should I be a Peep Show to massage your arrogant ego? My fault again for bullying you up, maybe I might change my mind. You will just have to be patient and hope it's worth the wait. G

 **I already knew you would not show me your nipples. I don't know you in person. I don't even know if it is you in the pictures, you sent to me? Then I realise you just like talking and not doing facts.**

 **You could be anyone, even a man. Taking pictures from the Internet, it's not that difficult. But I'm sorry for you, but I am not the kind of person who believes everything they are told.**

 18:37

Oh Luca, I'm honest, I am not a man, the pictures are mine what is the point of sending pictures that belong to someone else, when I hope, we are going to meet it would be a stupid thing to do. I have been told I was Liggio's daughter. so, you think that they are not my breasts, as you point out there could be anyone's if you see me in December then you will know if they are or not. when I arrive, I will text you give you my address and you can come into my bed, and we can Make Love all night the best sex you ever had Luca. You must believe that I am not playing some silly game. Look I sent a message to a contact in Corleone who offered me assistance if I needed it, he could vouch for me, just believe in yourself, I fancy the pants of you. You are a good-looking guy to me, maybe you just need a little push, maybe you are happier alone. Tell me if you have someone you are intimate with, if you have, she's a lucky bitch and I will leave you alone. Ok.

 **19:00**

Since you always mention this Salvatore, send him to me so I will have confirmation of what you say.

I thought you knew this guy is he not one of your friends? He lives in Corleone. Sorry I misunderstood, I thought he was a friend of yours. look to prove they are my breasts, I am ready to send a better photo, then you will see I am genuine, and this is not some sick joke at your expense. Gigliola.

I felt I had been manipulated into taking the following action, but I was infatuated besotted with Luca, he had to be mine I threw my dignity out of the window like some love-struck teenager I was going to give in to his demands. So, standing in front of the wardrobe with my mobile in hand I took two photographs of my naked breasts.

OK I understand this Salvatore will never come looking for me.

OK you want to show me.

Not perfect it shows the flash of the camera, I will try again tomorrow.

I really can't understand you.

I want to please you, you think I am a fraud, making fun of you, you say I am bullshit So I'm calling your bluff, how do I know you are not having a laugh at my expense? That you are not an honest sincere man but a womaniser who enjoys the thrill of some woman almost begging that you make mad passionate love to her. You were the man that once said when a decision is made it is not changed, but the fact you are once again exchanging messages with me proves you are a hypocrite, and not always true to your own word. Maybe it is a game to you, because you like most people in Corleone will hate me because I am Liggio's daughter.

I don't hear anyone, but I notice as soon as I told you to send me Salvatore, the photos arrived.

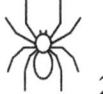 **21:32**

That was purely coincidence, I thought you knew Salvatore as we have already discussed; you said you didn't, I wanted to prove I was a woman and not some crazy bitch who hangs around on Facebook so she can have sex chats with gullible men like you for a laugh! I made friends with you because you live in Corleone the town that my parents came from, the town where I was conceived Corleone is a place that is very special to me. But not just because of that when I looked at your photographs there was an instant attraction. We have had a volatile friendship so far, but look at us we are once again talking, so that must mean something.

 **Booo.**

 So, we are back to the one-word answers. What does it mean. You can be so maddening at times; I just want to slap you.

 **You're violent then.**

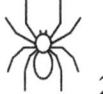 A slap Luca I would not class as violent. Getting a gun out and shooting someone like my father often did now that's violence. You're playing me, I don't like that. You know how much I want you, but you're too high and bloody mighty too arrogant. You will Make Love with me even

71

if I do have to put a gun to your head. So yes, I guess I am violent after all. I am coming to get you Luca Oliveri.

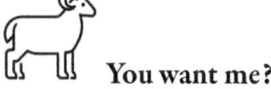 **You want me?**

That comment left me annoyed yet again. Did this man not listen to what was said to him? For weeks now we had talked of little else but having sex together the fact that seemed to have gone straight over his head, it really was like conversing with two different people!!!!!!

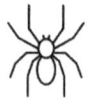 Don't play games Luca, you have known for weeks now that I want you.

 **For real?**

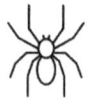 My God man what is wrong with you, what have you not understood after all this time??? Do you want me to put an advert in the newspaper, I Gigliola Castania Liggio, do hereby announce I would like to make mad passionate love to the shepherd of Corleone, who goes by the name of Luca Oliveri.

 **No, no newspapers.**

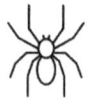 It was a joke Luca. I could shout it in the town

square to make you blush not that many would understand what I was shouting about, except maybe a few tourists who spoke English.

Oh, cause, it was lost in translation or was he not as simple as I sometimes believed him to be. I say this because I had never got round to try to photograph my nipples again, something Luca had not forgotten about and was keen to remind me of in the most subtle of ways.

 **I knew it was all a joke, from the beginning.**

Now it is a good night you have to give it to me with the photos of the nipples.

I went offline and sat contemplating if I was really prepared to do what he asked, my first attempt had been a disaster. Maybe that was no bad thing, flashing my breast to him was one thing it had never been full frontal just enough to keep his attention. I had never done anything like this before. I remember in 1992 I've been approached by a Scottish newspaper who had wanted me to do a full frontal in the paper, after I had been all over the media for an un- mafia related incident. I had of course turned them down even though they were willing to pay me. Now here I was deciding if I was going to flash my breasts to a complete stranger because I found him sexually attractive. now who was a hypocrite?

16/ 10/ 202

 **11:44**
Send the photo.

 11:09.

So, look here is Liggio's nipple. Now do you believe me?

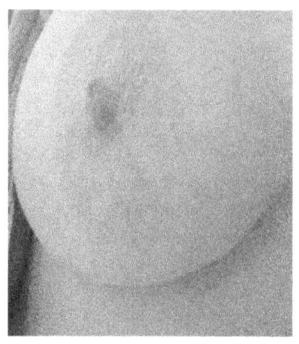

 It is beautiful.

Thank you, Luca, would you like to kiss them?

I got so excited the thought of your mouth your tongue caressing them, between my legs, I think I need a cold shower now, oh Luca.

 **12:30**

Why do you need a cold shower?

It's an English expression comment when someone thinks of making love with their lover, but they are not there, to dampen their passion, they say they need a cold shower. The coldness of the water shakes you from the passionate thoughts you are having. You don't actually have a shower. thinking about making love with you especially after you said how beautiful my breasts are, I got over excited hence the expression.

13:03

So, you wanna fuck with me?

Luca was really starting to try my patience, how many times did I have to say, yes, I want to fuck with you, until he begged to stop.

Yes, Luca at the moment yes, you're all I think about. But when I get to Corleone will I still feel the same? Maybe it's just a fantasy, maybe you are too naive for me? Since it has taken you so long to realise that my heart is set on seducing you.

17:13

Luca?

 **Yes.**

You will Make Love with me?

But if you don't even show up, how can I answer.
let me see you,
The face,
The body,
the breasts
everything
the whole picture of you.

No look forget it. It is not allowed; I cannot show my identity until the book is published. You decide when I come to Corleone. Goodbye

Goodbye.

I will miss our chats and of course you but I can still dream about you.

We always seem to be saying goodbye, but when it came to it, somehow, we always managed to go full circle I wondered how long it would be before we were talking again?

17:53

So, we have to say goodbye after all we have been through. You got me to show my breasts, even the close up of my nipple, it took a lot of courage for me to do that, but I did it because I care about you. I was grateful that you liked them it gave me a huge boost of self-confidence. I am no oil painting, but neither am I an old hag.

See for yourself.

 **If you have to remain anonymous, I can't help it.**

 I don't understand what you mean. Maybe you are some peasant shepherd with low morals, who thought you would chance your arm with the Godfather's daughter.

 18:51

In six weeks, I will be in Corleone and in your bed; so, you'd better get used to the idea.

19:06.
we'll see.

 21:05

I hope you don't mind if I have this picture on my desk, so I can look into those beautiful eyes while I write my messages to you.

This would not go down well, Luca seemed to be very protective of his identity, which I thought was a bit strange as he called me out on myself doing likewise, maybe he had something to hide? This made him even more appealing, was he your classic mafioso? Or was I letting my imagination run riot in my head.

You take pictures from my profile, but you don't send yours to me, you got a nerve, who said you could use my pictures I certainly didn't!

You're cross with me, as soon as I have had my makeover, I promise I will send you a photo of my face.

Goodnight my lover.

17/ 10/ 2021

11:22

I am the spider in her web, waiting for you to fall into my trap. I will wrap you in my silk, I will not eat you, but consume you with my passion oh Luca.

 **11:38**
Really.

12:39
And do you think I should be afraid?

 You should not have said you were afraid. I am a passionate gentle spider, but I can bite when I am angry.

Suddenly without warning Luca decided to talk about sex I thought was the spider about to capture her prey.

 **Do you like to fuck doggy style?**

Yes, with my bum stuck up in the air, I like to be finger fucked, I really enjoy that, I like to rotate my hips while the fingers are being pushed inside tickling my clitoris, that really gets me turned on, are you up to the job Luca?

We'll see.

Yes, we will. Do you have a preference?

The only preference I can have is to fuck your

79

arse, but you did tell me you don't like that.

 Maybe I could sit on top of you and wiggle my pussy on your cock. All this sex talk makes me want to fuck you even more. Are you sure you're willing to come into the spider's web.

 **Maybe you might let me into your arse.**

 No that will never happen, I think this is the end of our sexual friendship for me because I cannot be sure, that you would not try to take advantage, when I'm sexually aroused. I was once raped, the rapist stuck a beer bottle up my bum, so there is no way you're going to stick your cock up my arse.

 **But in fact, if you don't like that, I won't do it.**

 **15:33**

I thought you were an honest kind man, but underneath that beautiful smile there is a monster. You say you wouldn't force me to do what you prefer, but I would not be able to relax and enjoy myself, especially if I was on my knees, I would be powerless to stop you. I would feel no passion just disgust that you behaved like an animal. it is my own fault for talking to you in a sexual manner, but I felt a strong connexion with you.

 **It's not very nice thought you tell me I am a monster.**

however, at this point I don't think I have anything more to say to you.

 **15:52**

I wanted to call you a pervert but that would have been rude. It's not very nice and against human dignity to want to stick your cock up my arse. Not natural Luca you must see that as a Catholic, it is a sin against what is written in the Bible what should I think. I know I am the last person who should call you a monster when you think how my father behaved, but I feel physically sick at just the thought of it, it has tarnished what could have been a wonderful experience.

17/ 10/ 2021

 **14:52**

Ok, I don't care that much. Closed story now. From today I will not answer anymore, you have your messages.

Then block me the truth hurts. I know more than others how that feels. This spider is also on a mission. I will take revenge for your disrespect of me, this spider is coming to bite you with her venom, what has happened to us Luca?

 **You speak of respect to me**.

I have no respect for you. The woman who showed you her boobs, showed my nipples because I respected you, I wanted to prove I was genuine, I had great respect for you until you wanted ....

 **I didn't tell you I wanted.**

You asked me if I had any preferences and I answered you!! go and re read the message and you will see what I wrote to you.
YOU TOLD ME YOU DON'T LIKE IT. GO READ AGAIN AND SEE IF I DISRESPECTED YOU. YOU WHO WRITE MONSTER AND PERVERT.!!!!!!

I am sorry for you, but I know very well what respect is.

I of course remember the message from some time back, because I told you I didn't consider it normal unless you were in a gay relationship Luca are we falling out again, this is becoming a habit with us, we are like an old married couple squabbling. I'm sorry I was just a little shocked You made me laugh when you didn't understand the translation, once again I have failed to abide by the mafia mantra.

Laugh as much as you want but listen you can be whoever you want. But that doesn't mean you can afford to offend and laugh at people. You talk about respect so much you like respect and what's more you are hiding behind the photograph of the television actor to shamed to show your true identity, mafiosa.

Oh Luca, I was not laughing at you personally. Please, I just keep saying the wrong thing. We wanted to talk about unbridled passion if it really is over between us before we've even got started then just block me.

I will destroy my web and the fly can runaway escape from my silken thread. Is it such a shame we could have made such beautiful music together.

So do it, Luca, block me, unfriend me if you really have finished with me, disappear from my life forever. The press of a button, that is all it takes.

I was so confused this was not the first time he said I was hiding behind the profile of an actor, but when had I told him this? There was something not quite right, I re-checked our messages, but could find no mention of me ever saying my profile was an actor. I had been confused for a while now. I was sure that Luca had two concurrent profiles. At times he did seem like two different people as I've said before. it could explain why I found myself repeating things that we had already talked about it was all very strange.

17:24

Luca please, I'm not laughing making fun of you I said the wrong thing I insulted you I've tried to say I'm sorry. I have offended you that was not my intention I'm really sorry I appreciated you and your friendship Above all the talk about sex. I did hope we would become lovers, but it has all gone horribly wrong. Your angry and rightly so please can't we start over, if there is no answer by tomorrow evening, I will accept our friendship is really over.

 **19:22.**

Are you still angry with me, I'm really sorry I didn't mean to hurt you. Please Luca we were so close.

You may see it in your heart to forgive this stupid bitch. I am so sorry Luca.

 **I was angry with you!!!**

 22:00

Goodnight my dearest Luca.
18/ 10/ 2021

 **05:32**
Good morning

84

 Good morning

 17:32

Are you still angry with me?

 **Until you get forgiven yes.**

 And what prayers would you like me to do.

 **I don't want prayers.**

 I wasn't thinking about them. So, do you have something in mind anyway?

You will have to be the one to find a way to be forgiven.
See you all of you, would be a start.

 I guess it doesn't make sense to talk, if you won't forgive me until you see me.

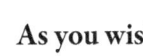 **As you wish.**

85

Well, if you won't forgive me what should a woman do but cry into her pillow.

Cry?
I see no reason.

Well, you won't forgive me, you break my heart that I will not look into those beautiful brown eyes you have, feel your lips on my naked skin.

You are a smart person, so you will find a way to
be forgiven, I'm sure.
I did not understand anything. anyway, do as you see fit.

Thank you for the compliment, but in the words of meatloaf, 'I will do anything for love, but I won't do that,' so I guess that's it.

17:58
OK
It all depends on you.

Oh, Luca don't be like that. We have had such lovely talks, I dreamed of crazy and passionate love with you, so this is it then. Bye tear up your photo and move on.

 **Ok.**

 So, we are done then? My hoped for lover Luca Oliver has abandoned me oh Luca Luca I am so sorry.

I was totally besotted, infatuated with this man. I was not going to give it up without a damn good fight, even if it meant giving into him, if I really cared about him, would I not want to please him. But could I really do that would my conscience allow such a thought to even cross my mind?

 Oh, Luca please I need you, I want you so much is it really over.

 **20:44**

I know you want to see me, but at the moment it's just not possible, so I guess you will have to go on being angry with me.

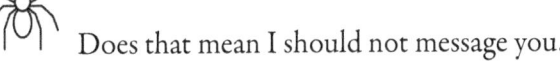 **Of course, I am angry, but not because I haven't seen you. But because of the names you called me your disrespect of me.**

 Does that mean I should not message you.

Stupid question if you're still mad at me you might very well not want to talk to me.

 If you let yourself be forgiven.

 So, what should I do? Have Anal sex with you.

 **But you do realise what you just wrote. Tonight, yes?**

 I'm not even in Sicily, so it would be a bit difficult. and I am sorry, but I would shoot you first rather than do that. you are not that handsome or sexy so go to hell, Luca Oliveri.

 OK, I understand that you have no interest.

 You will come back.

 **I do not think so.**

 Why are we fighting Luca? I was wrong, I said I'm sorry you're not a very forgiving person are you. I always end up giving you what you want. I am the one that will go to hell for committing a sin. Maria leggio said I'm not

Luciano's daughter she doesn't know anything was she even born in 86?

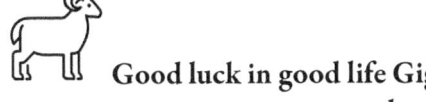 **Good luck in good life Gigliola Liggio, or whoever you may be.**

Once again, we were saying goodbye, I hoped this was just another empty gesture on Luca's part. He had previously backtracked, so I was hoping once his anger had subdued, he would see sense.

19/10/2021.
10:37.
Good morning, Luca.

 **Good morning.**

I decided not to draw attention to the fact he had gone against his own certainty that he would not change his mind but had, by saying good morning to me. Then again, I had known Luca long enough, to know that he was a very polite person whatever his other faults. he was always a well-mannered man.

I know you are still angry with me. I decided to block you it lasted only 5 minutes in the end I'm like a moth to a flame where you are concerned. Talking of flames did you say you like red hair?

 **Yes.**

Maybe I should get the hairdresser to dye my hair red, it is currently black. I like you very much Luca. I hope we can be friends.

 **Be seen with black hair first.**

As you wish.

If you write to me, I will reply even if I am angry with you.

Could I be forgiven? I hope to excite you, the thought of you taking off my clothes Thrills me.

22:09

Goodnight Luca now I'm going to bed to dream that you're taking off my red Lacy bra, I hope it becomes more than just a dream.

20/ 10/ 2021

 **05:52**

I like that even if you are angry with me, you still say good morning to me. My dream was amazing, you slipped off my bra, caressed and kissed my breasts each one in turn, then licked my nipples like you would an ice cream so they became erect with excitement. Passion consumed us both the sex was out of this world, sorry, God what are you doing to me.

 **Nothing I am just myself.**

 16:43

Did you miss me today hope my passionate outburst didn't embarrass you? But you shouldn't be so sexy for a shepherd.

 And how should I be?

 I guess if you are sexy, you can't do anything about it it's just the way you are.

 **Okay, I know you make fun of me, and I know I'm ugly.**

No Luca that's not true, believe me I am not mocking making fun of you. You are not ugly you have a sweet face and how can I not be captivated by those gorgeous brown eyes. Please believe in yourself do not put yourself down you are just as good as the next man.

 **If you say so.**

 I do Luca I mean what I say, when I say I dream of you, I am not as you would say making fun of you. I mean every word; I want to make mad passionate love with you. But your personal preferences made me a little nervous.

 **18:09.**
OK.

 **18:32.**

I am really 64 years old; I am the ugly one not you.

 **22:42.**

My flights have been cancelled again. I hope to come on the 6th of December. Goodnight Luca and don't get discouraged by other people.

21/ 10/ 2021.

Your flight is cancelled every two days.

 09:01

I'm glad you think it's funny I am furious at this rate I will
end up going by train from Milan, or worse still getting the
overnight ferry from Naples to Palermo.

 Ok, Patience.

 09:01

It is easy for you to say, covid is going crazy here again. there
is talk of another lockdown, Fate is determined I will not
return to Sicily. how is the flock? I love sheep.

11:52

why don't you tell me how many sheep you have? I'm not
going to steal then I'm just trying to get to know you as
a person and not just as a sex toy. Surely there is nothing
wrong with that. You still haven't told me if there is a
blacksmith in Corleone.

93

 **20:38**

So how is my favourite shepherd doing tonight can't wait to be back in Corleone.

 **I'm fine, thanks for the thought**.

 You are still angry with me. So, I will leave you alone.

 **22:30**

Goodnight, Luca.

23:01

So, no goodnight from you.

22/10/2021

17:57

Oh Luca, I miss talking to you is it so hard to believe. This is not some sick joke, do people make fun of you? Well not this person, I do want to be friends and see you in Corleone.

18:12
Oh Luca Luca.

19:44
What's up.

 You don't talk to me anymore.

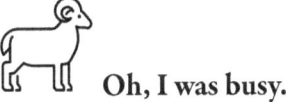 **Oh, I was busy.**

I am happy to know you were looking after my sheep.

This was the first time I referred to his flock as my sheep he never asked why I referred to his sheep as mine.

You are a man of few words; I hope you will be more talkative when we meet for a drink.

I came to the conclusion that Luca was quick to anger and could be very Moody. There was definitely a frosty atmosphere ever present between us at the moment. I knew he'd become upset when I referred to him as a monster, but I did my best to explain why I said that, and it was maybe not the choicest of words I could have used. Was he the kind of person that held a grudge. I decided to continue to message, if he did not want to read them, he could switch me off so to speak. I think secretly he liked the attention maybe it was a novelty to him to have a woman talking so openly about sex with him almost saying how much she desired his body. Boy I was giving him a hell of an ego, although he seemed to have a pretty big one already.

 22:18
Goodnight, Luca.

 **23/ 10/ 2021**
11:15
Good morning.

 Thank you, Luca.

 **You're welcome.**

18:32

In an effort to impress you I searched for the breed of sheep you have in my flock. So, when we meet for a drink that's if we are back on an even keel by then. We can talk about the sheep by the way I think they are the Pimizirita Breed.

 19:02

You are too informed to be a woman.
I think you really are a man!!!!!

Oh Luca, no no definitely a woman. I hope you are not suggesting that because I am bright enough to know what kind of sheep are in the flock, that I must in fact be a man? That is a very sexist thought to have. The Internet is a wonderful tool for learning, it's amazing what you can look up on there.

Oh Luca, not long now then you can see a picture of me, and you will see that I am very much a woman and that those big beauties are really mine. Then I am sure I will be forgiven finally I will come to Corleone. Share your bed, where we will make such beautiful music together.

 **OK.**

 22:28

Goodnight to my sexy shepherd.

 **Goodnight.**

 Thank you, Luca.

24/ 10/ 2021

 **15:26**

I'm pleased to see you have been busy I have done some ploughing in my time with an Oliver tractor. So, I could do some ploughing and you could pay me in kind as they say.

 **And how does this payment in kind work?**

Well, I work for you, and in return instead of being paid with money can you give me your body. But alas you still don't love me, you still think I am a man so I suppose it would be the money anyway have you got time to be on here have you done all your ploughing?

 **No.**

You are really kidding me I have looked at your pictures remember I hope when I get you, you will not be turned off by me?

24/ 10/ 2021

18:31
I have two photos of you now I'm not sure which one I prefer.

But with want permission do, you take my photos?

OK sorry but how can I help it if you're distracting me. Are you in a mood again I won't bother you anymore then we will no longer be lovers, I will find myself a mafioso in Palermo bye Luca we could have been so good together. It is your loss not mine.

OK.

So here we were again completing another circle. Luca obviously still angry with me still in a mood. At times we

99

*were both like school children in the playground. If we
did get to meet it would be a true miracle definitely an
act of God, was fate destined to bring us together? What I
couldn't understand was if he really wanted nothing to do
with me why didn't he just go offline, block me as far as I
was concerned, but maybe he was on one hell of an ego trip?
But now I decided I would play along; Did he get some kind
of perverse pleasure from our little spats bizarrely.*

So that's it then it all ends with an OK, I guess you
must have women in a queue waiting to jump into your bed.
For once Liggio's daughter is put in her place.

Who knows.

*This man could at times be so arrogant, was that his
character, or was I making him this way? That last
comment was like a red rag to a bull, I was straight onto the
defensive, determined to try and knock him off the pedestal
I had so gallantly put him on.*

You're probably shit in bed anyway and wouldn't
satisfy a demanding woman of my age. All this because I
downloaded a couple of your photographs you should be
flattered. Oh Luca, I'm sorry I take it back it was cruel I
just don't take rejection very well.

The truth is I want you so badly, but you will never be
mine, I just wanted a photo of you, to be desired again I
am sorry.

18:53

I don't want a mafioso, as, the saying goes, been there done that got the T-shirt. I want only you, but Gigliola with a big mouth has killed it this time I'm sure of that. Yet again I am sorry, so so sorry.

 21:15

One last thing, you tell anyone in Corleone, that I showed my breasts, and almost begged you for sex, you will feel the full force of a mafiosa, and I will extract revenge the like of, you will never have nor will ever see again.

25/ 10/ 2021

06:30
Are you threatening me?

Oh Mr Oliveri, sweet Luca, why would I want to threaten you? This all started because I took a couple of your pictures from your profile page, because I adore you. Want to look at your smiling face on my desk, I cannot help it if I find you so sexually attractive with your weight, I would have thought you'd be grateful, I have given you a second chance. We have shared such intimate thoughts. I have shown you numerous photos of my breasts because I wanted you to know I really was a woman, who wanted you so badly it hurts. Because I hoped it would make you want me too.

10:29

So, no answer! It could be you are busy; are you really in a mood and consider we are no longer friends?

 **I just hope you are beautiful and are good in bed.**

 Oh, look you have replied was that an invitation? I am no Miss World, but nor do I look like the back end of one of your cows. I have been told I am exciting in bed, you will not want to leave, if you do succumb and grant me access to your desirable body.

 **OK.**

 13:36

I see you remove me from your friends list OK, no problem, do what you want!!!!!

 I have already re friended you half an hour ago. I thought that's what you wanted me to do are you still mad at

102

me even more so because I downloaded some of your photos and I had not asked first. I did think we were making up. I have to feed my Ravens, but I will message later and grovel if that's what you want.

What are you doing? You blow hot and cold I have no idea what's going on do you still think I'm laughing making fun of you? Why should I be hypocritical show you my full breasts if I just wanted to make fun of you, that was an intimate thing to do, and something I have told you I have only ever done once before. maybe I should just find someone else to want. The problem is I really want you, after 26 years you are the one, I want in my bed to kiss and caress to play with my body, to make me feel all those beautiful feelings again, to share the intimacy between two people. Oh, Luca I never wanted anyone as much as I want you and I would even include the mafioso in that statement.

I was really confused. After all this time, if he really thought I was a man why would he talk sex with me, did he really swing both ways, was he bisexual? And if he was how would I feel about that.

OK you have said you will come right. This means that when I see you, if I come, I will decide

whether to have sex with you or not.

 **15:19**

I guess that's fair enough, I'm not going to implode, yes, we will forget about your attraction, sex isn't really important to me. Hell, I've not had sex since 1994, so I obviously haven't missed it. the mafioso was pretty hot so who knows you maybe will not live up to my expectations, I don't mean that in a malicious way.

 Then you won't have sex with me?

 Look Luca, I'm not the most beautiful woman in the world. I am not some Sophia Loren look alike. You sound pretty strict about your sexual partners and how they look, so I think I'm fresh out. Not only that you're still convinced that I am a man.

 **Okay do what you like.**

If I do what I want, I will take you to bed. You will have no say in the matter, I would prefer not to have to put a gun to your head, but you know Luca what they say about Sicilian women.

104

 **No, I don't know what Sicilian women say.**

 There is a saying that Sicilian women are more dangerous than a rifle. if you have your fields ploughed, will you be planting wheat or barley? Then I don't know why I'm asking because you are not going to tell me.

 **16:24.**
Just think when I walk into that square, when you see me then you might regret refusing me.

 **Ok**

 16:50
So, one last thing before I disappear, if I turn out to be half decent in view of your high standards, would you make passionate love to me?

 **I have not understood.**

 17:14.
You said it would depend on how beautiful I am if you would take me into your bed. If you consider that I am not ugly, will you allow me the pleasure of having your penis entertain me. or am I really wasting my time is it you the one

105

that is doing the teasing? It would have been so wonderful, your rough hands caressing my body. I'm sorry if I have embarrassed you, but you were the one that said you like licking a woman's pussy and then putting your fingers in there.

 **I am not embarrassed but I haven't seen you. If you show up, I can tell you if I like you or not.**

 Once I've seen the hairdresser had my hair dyed, I will send a photo, so I know before I arrive in Corleone If you consider I am desirable or not.

 **As you wish.**

 **20:56**
You can be so maddening, let's just forget it. Fancy yourself. Will it be, (a) as you wish, (b) shrug of the shoulders, or (c) Ok?
Goodnight Luca.

 **Goodnight.**

26/ 10/ 2021

 **10:26**
I had a long chat with Giovanni about it this morning about

the way I have been behaving especially towards you he's very disappointed in me. I am in myself I belong in the gutter like Gianni said. The spider has lost her web, so now you are free the fly has escaped my sexual advances.

 18:30.
I will miss talking to you.

 22:37
Goodnight, friend.

27/ 10/ 2021

 12:29
Hope the bad weather in Sicily did not affect the farm too much and that my sheep are all ok.

 **Do not worry.**

 I'm not worried why should I worry about you and your farm. The weather forecast is predicted to snow for us in a couple of weeks does it snow in Corleone.

 **No, it's not snowing.**

19:02

Good evening, Luca.

 **Good evening to you.**

I was amazed he had answered but I knew Luca well enough by now to know he was just being polite so I should not get too excited.

 **20:50**

I know you are still angry with me; you have every right to be goodnight, Luca.

28/ 10/ 2021

 10:38

Good morning, Luca.

 **21:04**

So, are you never going to talk to me again? Guess I will not be seeing you when I come to Sicily then.

22:19

I never had you down as a childish person. I'm now glad

you don't want to Make Love with me. I need a man not some child from the school playground.

30/ 10/ 2021

 **09:20**

Oh Luca.

You are loving this power you have over me. Just because your life can go on as before, while you wait for me to arrive in Corleone. Then I have to try and charm you into bed, and you will serve me like your stallion does the mare.
Maybe I will just have to overcome the loss, after all one cock is very much like another.

 **10:28.**

It is reciprocal, especially when hiding behind a fake photo.

 That's why you act like a child all because of a photograph? I have six weeks to get over you, you're mad and so Moody anyway I'm better off giving you a wide berth.

 **OK**

 I didn't mean that, I like you as a person. You will get a photograph of me as soon as I'm able to send you one.

109

it would seem the roles are reversed you are now the spider, and I am the fly caught in your web, while you decide what you're going to do with me.

 20:21

Oh Luca, luca luca, please, talk to me Luca.
20:55

 I decided when I send you my photo you must see me in a state of undress, so red lace bra suspender belt, lacy pants, my fancy black stockings made to measure if that doesn't do the trick then you had better hold out for the next Miss Sicily.

 Thank you, goodnight lover.

 Goodnight.

For a change it was me giving a thumbs up.

31/ 10/ 2021

 **11:08**

Good morning, Luca.

At some stage I must have un- friended him again judging by my next message to him.

 **11:48**

Thank you for accepting my friend request. It means a lot to me. Are you really starting to forgive me? You are really under my skin; I would fall from the stars into your arms.

 **16:00**

I wonder if you would be offended, if I sent you romantic thoughts. I guess you're still angry with me as you haven't said yet that I am forgiven.

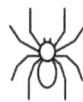 **16:23**

That's a no then? Okay I just want to say good night and good morning then Luca, to be polite until you decide what you really want to do.

 **Why do you just keep repeating the same things over and over.**
I guess because hiding behind the fake photo isn't bad.

 You and that damned photo, yes, I keep repeating the same things over and over, because you still don't seem to understand why I'm hiding behind that photo. I'm just a bullshitter, a man having a laugh at your expense, maybe I get

some perverse pleasure from chatting men up on Facebook. Maybe I am a gay man then you turn me on. if that's what you want to believe I can't change your mind, so what's the point, why should I really care. as they say there are plenty of fish in the sea, I am sure there are plenty of single men in Corleone that might give me the pleasure of their cock.

 **OK.**

You and that God damn Ok. I realise now I am wasting my time, you just led me on a merry dance. well Mr Luca Oliveri it's not cute it's not funny. you once said you would never make fun of anyone, not only are you arrogant but you're also a liar as well!!!!!!

NOVEMBER

01/ 11/ 2021

10:56
Good morning, Luca.

Good morning.

Thank you.

 **You're welcome.**

 23:09

So, what does my favourite shepherd look like today? Hope you have got all your ploughing done, now to Harrow ready to plant. I hope you are looking after my sheep. I have been looking at some sexy underwear to get your pulse racing goodnight, Luca.

02/ 11/ 2021

 **12:15**

Sorry about all the thumbs up caught the button. I have not lost the plot. Hope you are well? I am working on my new book, better it ends while I am still able to work. Wishing I was back in Corleone. red or black underwear, I so want to excite you.

 **14:27**

Oh, Luca red or black?

 Red like fire.

 **18:00**

Oh Luca, it looks like you're a passionate man. I had better look to see if I can get some red fishnet stockings.

 19:14

Do you like this before I buy it?

SENT IMAGE OF BABYDOLL SET.

 **Yes.**

 Then I will buy it just in case my luck is in. I would love you to take it off me.

 That is fine.

 **23:35**
Goodnight Luca.

It would seem Luca was still mad with me apart from the brief answers he'd given to the questions I'd asked there

114

were no messages, so I thought why bother.

04/ 11/ 2021

 Have you missed me Luca?

05/ 11/ 2021

 **10:55**

Good morning.

 **Good morning.**

 Thank you.

 You're welcome.

 **19:07**

So, my sexy shepherd I hope you have had a good day? I hope the flock is okay. Do you have a sheepskin rug, or do I need to buy one?

 **No I have no carpets sheepskin or otherwise.**

Well, I will have to buy a large sheepskin rug in Palermo then. Just in case I meet your high standards, I so wanted you naked upon it. Oh Luca Oliveri!!!!!!!

 **Me naked?**

Oh yes Luca, you naked on the sheepskin, the feeling of sheepskin offered against bare skin is so sexy.

 **So, you won't be undressed with me?**

 Oh Luca, I will let you undress me, then we will both lay naked on the sheepskin and as you have previously said have wild unbridled sex.

 **Nice.**

 Nice!! I had an English teacher once hated the word nice, he said it should be struck from the dictionary.

Somethings he said are beautiful or ugly they are never nice. And anyway, at the present it is just a dream a fantasy you may not find me sexually pleasurable.

 **I can't know this.**

 Soon you will see me as I really am, I am ready for rejection, I can still fantasise if it is a no.

 I have not understood.

 Well, if you find me unattractive, and cannot see yourself making love with me. I can console myself with my dreams until I get over you.

 OK.

 Goodnight, Luca, would you be my lover? I won't let you down, given the chance to prove I can give you a good time in bed. I am not fooling you; I think you are a great guy. I so want to ravish you.

 **23:35**
Goodnight.

06/ 11/ 2021

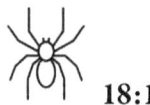 **18:16**

Good evening, Luca. We had thunderstorms last night; I had an erotic dream about us. We were both naked on the sheepskin, we explored each other's bodies then made love, passionate love oh Luca it was so beautiful.

 **Good.**

 Good Luca? Is that all you can say. If we do get together, I hope you say a little bit more than good. Do you have a single or a double bed?

Things it seemed were not good between us. The chats we had previously had now seem to have dried up. If there was a response it was usually one or two words, very concise to the point that was it.

07/ 11/ 2021

 **12:29**

Good morning, Luca, hope you are keeping well?

13:00
Good.

 13:45

Still a man a few words. I hope when we meet our lips are locked in a passionate kiss.

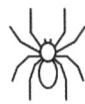 **19:04**

So how was your day? My favourite shepherd. I guess we will not be going for a horse ride after all. It won't be long now before you can see me in all my glory.

Good.

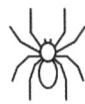 Oh Luca, I was hoping you would ask if I would be naked. Maybe I will wear that little red number try to get you excited. I am going for a bath:Do you prefer a bath or a shower.

Both.

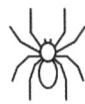 Do you have a large bath which two people could fit into? Have you ever shared it bath with a woman? I have sent snake emojis because I want to wrap my body around

yours. Oh Luca, I will be excited for hours.

 **22:12**

I am sorry Luca; I will stop with the sexual innuendos it is not fair. But I will send the photo as promised as soon as I have had my Gigliola makeover.

 **OK**

 **22:47**

Oh Luca, I hope we can meet as friends for a drink? I know that conversation will be difficult, but we can try and talk about my sheep.

08/ 11/ 2021

 08:30

Good morning.

 **Buon giorno.**

 Oh Luca, have a good day.

 15:10

Hope you had a good day? I might be a so-called mafia Princess, but I don't mind getting my hands dirty, you see I could be an asset to you on the farm and not just in the bedroom.

 **I did not understand anything.**

 I hope we meet when I come to Corleone, I meant I could help on the farm. then maybe it is not your farm, and you just work there?

 15:37
Maybe.

 17:44

I'm only interested in the shepherd not the farm. Do you have tea in your kitchen, or should I bring my own? Just in case I'm invited for a ride!!! Excuse me Luca, a ride on horseback.

17:44
Ok.

18:46

I hope you're more talkative if we meet for a drink, do you like red hair?

19:10

Okay Luca forget it if you don't care, well just Remember Me.

Either red or black.

My hair is both, too bad you will not get to see it now, I bet you say OK.

And what can I tell you?

You won't tell me anything, because you are suspicious of me. Do not trust me with my past, I can understand that.

20:34
And, therefore?

122

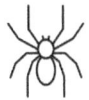 I've just taken a bath as I was relaxing in the bubbles, I realised that I assume you are alone up in the mountains of Corleone. In reality you could be the local stallion so to speak, a different woman every day. While you are trying to find the woman, you want to spend your life with. So, I guess I have little chance with you, with my looks my age, but I have my fantasies of you, and they see me through these cold nights.

 **Good fantasy is needed in life**.

 21:13

Did I forget to ask if you're still mad at me? I will have you Luca and not only in my fantasy.

 23:05

Goodnight lover of my dreams.

09/ 11/ 2021

 **05:59**

Good morning.

 10:59

Wow you get up early, you make me feel really lazy. Good job

I'm not a farmer's wife. Don't panic Luca it was just a generic comment.

 18:28

How is my favourite shepherd/ farmer? I do hope I get to meet you. Are you far from the town?

 **Fine thanks.**

 Do you have a Christmas tree? I have a little gift for you to hang on it it has your name on it.

 **No, no Christmas tree.**

 **21:39**

No, well I will have to change that.

No!

22:24

Goodnight my fantasy lover, now I'm going to bed to fantasise about making mad passionate love with you. I hope you will like it, when we do it for real?

 **Buonanotte.**

10/ 11/ 2021

 11:13

Good morning, Luca have a nice day. As you like red, I will send a photo with me wearing my red velvet dress, it is a wraparound style so easy to take off I will bring it with me.

 **Fiery red??**

 11:30

Oh, Luca are you very passionate? Taking you to bed, making mad passionate love to you. I am passionate, then you might have already garnished this from what I have said.

 **I wait for the photo**.

 18:46

So, how's my sexy shepherd doing tonight? I hope you've had a good day. Not a good day for me, my book will not be ready for printing before I come to Sicily. Covid is also a worry.

 **19:26**
Understood.

 **23:11**
Goodnight lover of my dreams Luca.

11/11/2021.

 **11:36**
Oh Luca, no goodnight, no good morning, ok, goodbye.

 **Goodbye.**

I was furious, the arrogance of this man. just like that he was saying goodbye. no explanation, I had said it to him first, but he had barely been talking too me for days. We were on the downward spiral again, and I wasn't going to help matters I get as you know vitriolic.

 It's your loss anyway you were probably rubbish in bed. I need a real man not pathetic shepherd, then it was never going to happen anyway, you're all talk Luca Oliveri, it was just a fantasy in your head I would never have met your

high standards. You are one of those men that is good talking a good fuck but when it actually comes to it, you're like a little boy lost.

So, if I'm rubbish, why don't you go fuck yourself, you have broken me!!!!

I am sorry how have I broken you? Don't be so melodramatic, the younger one who's been in the mood, angry with me, so long ago I cannot recall what I had actually done to make you so mad, all I wanted to do was just to Make Love with you, you excite me, I am very sexually attracted to you.

I don't see why?

No Luca so again putting yourself down, poor sad put upon Luca. how many times this is not some sick joke, I do find you very attractive. That mean and Moody look you always seem to have in a bizarre way is somehow attractive. You never seem to smile, are you really such an unhappy man? When you talk in your messages, you sound like a kind sincere man who does have a passionate side, then of course there is those beautiful brown eyes. Damn it Luca, I care about you, and you know, it's not just a quick romp in bed if that's what's worrying you? If I hurt you in anyway, I am sorry that was never my intention. but at times you can be so infuriating.

127

I realised that no matter what I now said, Luca was not going to listen let alone talk to me. He had totally switched off; it was up to me to try and get him back onside, so we could complete the circle once again. But I had the feeling this time it was not going to be easy.

 Oh Luca, we shared such intimate thoughts. We were once so close. Please I'm not mocking you, you're really in my head please Luca talk to me...... once you see me in my red dress you will forgive me.

I don't want to break you:I want a night like you said a night of wild passion I want you inside of me Luca Oliveri. Will I be lucky enough to have you?

 13:16

Not to worry Luca, guess it's back to the mafiosi then? They usually fuck anyone.

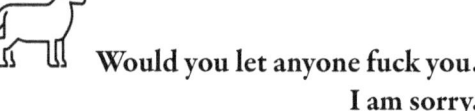 **Would you let anyone fuck you.
I am sorry.**

 No Luca, I am Liggio's daughter, and I am furious with you. I have said many times I don't show my chest to just anyone. but I see now in the end you coerced me, you were the one playing the game, knew exactly what to do. Like these men that groom young girls, you did that to me only I am an older woman. Maybe because of that, that's why I succumbed in the end. You are a much younger man

that wanted to see me naked. But then I did have a strong sexual attraction to you, so it seemed a natural thing to do. I appreciated the way you openly talked to me about sex when in reality we were complete strangers. You did not know me as a person, nor did I know you. I thought we had a strong connection, maybe it seems I was mistaken, foolish old woman, who still thinks she's 26 in her head. It is you who has broken me, not as you suggested I who have broken you.

 14:33.

You might think it, but I am not a whore. I am very loyal. I believe that 26 years of sexual abstinence, because I yearned for Valerio proves that. If you took me into your bed, why would I want anyone else but you screwing me? It seems the Fly has escaped the spider and her web.

Luca was really trying my patience, one minute he was jealous I might sleep with anyone, then he was suggesting I would not sleep with him either. I wanted to scream, sometimes it seemed he was deaf to what I said to him!!!!

Luca, I don't understand you? I thought you decided you did not want to sleep with me, because you consider I am a loose woman and will sleep with any man if it is offered to me. Because you think I will not sleep with you. Make up your mind Luca.

Do you want to take me to your bed or not? Decide before I come to Corleone. If it is yes, I swear on my life I will be faithful and loyal to you. Oh Luca, I would get down on my knees and pray. Please forgive me, we would have been so good together, even if it had only been the once. Then I guess I never thought you cared that much anyway.

 I won't give up, maybe the photo in my red underwear will save me. I never ever meant to hurt you, you are not just a shepherd you are a sexy shepherd, a kind warm sincere man and no I am not teasing you, I mean every word I say to you. Gigliola.

 **15:03**

So, the word is goodbye it makes no difference how the tears are cried it's over...... I can make believe you need me when it's over....

I will leave you alone, but I'm here, only for you Luca.

 **19:03**

I am such a fool, please Luca I'm really sorry, can we not start over? Just saying now if that's what you really want? Gigliola.

12/ 11/ 2021

 **10:54**

Good morning, Luca.

Good morning.

130

12:45

Oh Luca, you have made my day. You are a wonderful man; I mean it and thank you once again.

 **21:42**

I thought you should see me in real time, so I gave in, and video called, then got cold feet and hung up especially as you are really mad at me, maybe by Monday, I will have overcome my apprehension. Gigliola.

 **23:03**

Goodnight my dearest Luca.

13/11/2021

 Good morning, Luca.

19:07

I decided the only way Luca was going to respond, was if I let him see me. So, I sent a photo of me wearing my red shirt, as I knew he liked red, and one of me with my trilby on.

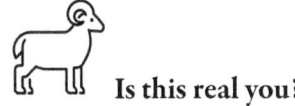 **Is this real you?**

 Yes, this is Gigliola Castania Liggio, so do you like me.

So now you have seen me complete with red highlights.

 **OK**.

 Okay? is that all you can say!!! Guess I am not up to it then.

 **About what?**

 If I am good enough to go to bed with? Ok Luca I always knew it would be a no. I'm far too good for you anyway, because I have a brain and can think for myself. I guess you prefer women who cower down to you.

 **I said nothing.**
You say everything as usual.

 I'm sorry, I believed it was love at first sight for me to flash my breasts then my nipples, what wank yourself off

looking at them. Then it is goodbye.!!!

 **I have three weeks available to me, let's see if you can convince me.**

I knew what Luca was suggesting, he was a clever man, and in my vulnerable state, he knew he could manipulate me. It would seem he was the real spider; I was the fly powerless to be caught in his web.

 No Luca, I am not playing this game anymore. I will not be a peep show for your enjoyment. Yes, you're cute, with your mean and moody look, those beautiful brown eyes, but I have gone 26 years without sex, I have not missed it, until I met you, but I can go a while longer.

 **21:13.**
It's a shame really Luca, but you are making fun of me, playing some cruel game. This is not very kind, maybe you are not the sincere kind shepherd I thought you to be?

14/11/2021

 **12:18.**
Luca, good morning. Look I am sorry for how I have behaved, no wonder you see me as a whore. I am not like that really. I just got carried away, suddenly feeling those emotions again after so long. But surely, we can be friends

can we not. Like normal people on Facebook. You I am sure must be terribly embarrassed by the way I have behaved when messaging you. I can only yet again say I am so sorry. Gigliola.

 **So, you don't want to take me to bed anymore?**

 Of course, I do Luca, but I feel as if I have come across as some crazy slapper. I'm trying to give you an excuse to opt out.

 **Rest assured I know how to defend myself.**

 I'm sorry Luca, I am not threatening you. What do you think I'm going to do, take you to bed, then do a Liggio, pull a gun out and blow your brains out. What do you think of me? Not much it would seem, it's not my fault Liggio might have been my father.

 **Too many problems fail you.**

 15:04
Luca, I want you so bad it hurts. I want to feel your hands sliding down my body, caressing my breasts, the only reason

I was mad about you having a hairy chest, was because I wanted to be able to slide my tongue down it, as it made its way down to your penis. I was told by the mafioso, I was a horny bitch. I just want to Make Love with you, to feel your fingers caressing my clitoris. If we do see each other in Corleone maybe they will be a spark, you cannot deny we have chemistry between us. I know how I want you so much, but until you see me in person you might not feel the same, I have to prepare myself for rejection.

 **We will see what happens.**

 I am confident we will become lovers, you will love every minute of it, I will give you the ride of your life, so much so that you will want it again and again.

 **16:22**

Here I go again talking dirty, embarrassing you no doubt and having to apologise yet again. I really should put my brain into gear before I open my mouth. Think what I'm going to say before I say it. goodness what must you think of me? But I cannot get past the thought of being naked with you. I have to ask; do you have a big firm penis Luca? I want to feel it inside of me, thrusting back and forth. I can get very vocal, very wet when sexually aroused.

 **How much do you want it?**

Oh Luca, more than words can say. I'm crazy about you and your manhood.

 **But you have not seen my penis.**

 Luca Oliveri you know full well I have not seen it. That does not mean I cannot fantasise about it. You have seen my breasts, what about you showing me your penis when he is firm and erect. Oh, but this is just a joke to you, make fun of the Godfather's daughter.

 **I don't understand what you mean. I am not making fun of anyone.**

 17:26

You know exactly what I mean but never mind. I hope when we meet there is a physical attraction, which then leads to sexual desire between us. you seem to me to be a warm and sincere person with genuine feelings that must not be trodden on.

 **18:33**

Learn Italian because I don't know English and I want to be able to talk to you in my own language.

 I am learning Italian, but I will not be able to speak fluently in three weeks, not only that but will we have time to talk Luca, if we are in bed together will we not be preoccupied with other things.

Of course.

 You have really excited me at the prospect of us being together up close and personal, but more importantly naked. Oh, Luca Oliveri what are you doing to me.

Send me some more photos of yourself; maybe where I can see you in full with your clothes on.

He was starting to turn the screw a little bit tighter, making suggestions, knowing full well that I would ultimately succumb and give in to his request.

 I'm pleased to see you're happy enough to see me fully clothed. I will give it some thought; At the moment I am semi naked and going to take a bath.

If you want to, even without your clothes on that's okay for me.

You don't want to see me naked, not with my body, I'm a bit like your curvy friend from Turin.

Of course, I did not want him to see me in full. I feared he would be put off by what he saw, I needed to entice him into my web by words alone at the moment. Get him sexually motivated, so that he would not be able to resist me when he eventually did see me as a whole person in reality. At least I could console myself with the thought that he did in fact find my breasts very desirable.

I thought to myself, he was very clever, gently making the suggestion because he knew how much I really wanted to please him. But I had to box clever to get around this particular request.

**Send the photo anyway.
Come on I am glad to see you naked.**

No, no, even Liggio's daughter has standards, if you sent one of yourself naked, I might agree then.

**20:45
I have not understood.**

20:11

Oh yes you have Luca you undress, send me a naked photo

139

with your penis erect, then I send a naked photo all length in return.

I was soon to learn do not try to pull the wool over the eyes especially when the man in question happens to be a shepherd. I was so certain he would not agree I was so wrong.

 **Do you want my dick?**

The next thing I knew the photo arrived not taken from a very good angle. The problem was all I could focus on was the two layers of fat that encompassed Luca's midriff, then behind these two mountains of flab, I could just about make his penis standing behind them. I was shell shocked, before I knew it he'd remove the photo so I never really got a good look at it, his penis that is.

 **Not that great. you don't like it do you?**

I knew how sensitive he was about his penis so I could not slap him in the face and be truthful. But it was not what I'd expected but being so shocked by how overweight he was, especially as he was a farmer shepherd who will be very active most of the time. I couldn't really give an honest opinion I had no option, then to do a Pinocchio.

 **Now send a picture of you.**

Sorry Luca, cannot be done, come on you have seen my breasts, my nipples on more than one occasion, you can only see the rest of me when you take me to bed.

You are not of your word.
at this point I will not write to you anymore.
I knew I couldn't trust you, and I trusted you. it turned
out what I thought was right, I cannot trust you and
therefore the game ends now!!!!

I wasn't deceiving you Luca; I was so sure you were not going to send a photo; you took the wind out of my sails but thank you he's magnificent.

Yes, that you have deceived me is a good thing,
and that I was sure of it, and you have it for me confirmed.

As a mafioso you have to show respect yourself before going to bed, I will show that respect by sending you a picture of my vagina as I will respect the code that Giovanni taught me to follow. so that I can prove you can trust me.

 **Okay, doesn't matter anymore. I don't care anymore.**

 Oh, Luca I won't worry about it then.

 **22:52**

My dearest Luca, I know you said you no longer cared, but I wanted to prove that you were wrong. That you can trust me, but the light is not right, so I will try in the morning when I'm in bed and there is natural sunlight, my bedroom is very dark even when the main light is on, I cannot stop thinking about your wonderful cock goodnight.

15/ 11/ 2021

 **11:04**

Good morning, Luca.
I am really sorry I did try, but alone it's not easy. I need one of those selfie sticks my arm is just not long enough. I still can't believe you actually sent the photo, I dreamt about your dick last night.

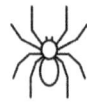 **17:15**

Oh, Luca what have I done, you are an honest man. I have been very selfish in thinking about my wishes, without any thought of how it might affect you. You've always been so distant two-word answers, or just an emoji, then yesterday you did something out of character. Please don't get me wrong, your cock is beautiful I would Make Love with you tomorrow if I could. But I am worried that we will open a door that we cannot close, we have no idea of the consequences should we become intimate, which path it might lead us down, are we both prepared for what might befall us.

I had no idea at the time just how significant that last message would turn out to be.

17:45
Luca talk to me, should we just forget it everything all together?

**For me it is a closed thing.
Your game is over.**

It was never a game to me, I wanted you, but it seems like you're the only one playing. Show me your dick, get me all sexually aroused then shut it down. Luca I will have you now, even if I do have to put a gun to your head. You want to see me naked; I will relent then you will win I will show you my vagina, that's what you really want to see, just block me if I am mistaken, then like you say the game will be over.

143

18:24

Honesty time I am really 65 fat and ugly so I would never have had the chance of bedding you. You were the one trying to coerce Me into sending you a picture of my pussy, that's what you really wanted to see. You're the one playing games, get some perverted enjoyment from taking advantage of vulnerable older women. Make you feel good, does it? The selfie stick will be here Wednesday so then you will see my pussy in all its pathetic glory. You better not laugh at me, you will see my bad Liggio genes, are you happy now Mr Oliveri.

 19:10

We are finished, I've decided I will not be browbeaten by some country shepherd with delusions of grandeur. I am not that desperate for a fuck with the likes of you, overweight, Moody a liar. You don't deserve my time. Your cock Would never have satisfied me anyway pathetic little man.

I am a hypocrite, Luca was right I hadn't stuck to my word, but that was because I was sure he wouldn't send me a photograph. I realised now that it didn't matter what I said Luca was not going to respond, he had stuck to his side of the bargain. I on the other hand had not, the only way to put things right was to honour the agreement. Even if I felt shame and disgust at what I was going to do.

 20:23

As a so-called woman of honour, I have to be seen to abide by the agreement that I made to you. I will send a photo you have asked for as a mark of respect to you, only God knows why I should respect the likes of a pervert like you to start with.

There is no need to send a photo now it is no longer of any use.

So, it was just a game, someone else showing you, there vagina. Don't need to see mine anymore. Why say you wanted to fuck me? Do you really get off on this, how many other women do you groom like this? You have said you can't trust me; This is my way of proving to you that you can. You were so intimate yesterday what happened to us in 24 hours? Oh, then silly me, there never was an us was there? You loved it the stupid bitch Desperate for your cock. Oh, what's the point, but I will send a picture anyway just to prove that unlike you I am not a liar and when I make an agreement, I do stick to it!!!!!!!

For as you can see, the photo is no longer needed! You did not keep your word this was enough the rest does not count anymore.

I have tried to explain Luca that you can sit on a chair, displaying your penis and take a photo on your mobile with one hand, I have to try and get it in the right position, hold the camera with one hand and tried to get my vagina in frame blind. it is not bloody easy believe me.

 **22:49**

Goodnight, Luca Oliveri.

 23:14

Luca alright to be in one of your moods, okay you are angry with me, but have I not just tried to explain myself. I notice you might not be replying, but you are reading my messages, you're loving this aren't you. I acted in a shameful way brought disrespect onto myself with these acts of madness. Dragging myself into the gutter where Gianni said I belonged. Letting my desire to make love with a Sicilian one more time, cloud my judgement. It started with me just wanting sex from you, but then I realised I wanted more, but I took the wrong path, now I awake from the fantasy, you are nothing like the mafioso. He might have been a bad man in his profession, but he was kind and gentle with me. Showed me what love was really all about not an arsehole like you. You who has taken advantage of maybe not just me, but other women as well to satisfy like your belly your oversized ego.

16/ 11/ 2021.

My selfie stick had been delivered but as there was no contact from Luca, I assumed that meant that this time he was not just in a mood. That he was definite in his decision that it was over between us but I had fallen for him. He consumed every hour of my day and was ever present in my dreams I was going to take a calculated risk, but I had nothing to lose if it all went pear shaped. But first I decided I was going to tell him the truth about why I had taken so long to respond when he sent his naked photo.

17/ 11/2021

 12:21

I was going to spare your feelings, but I feel it needs to be said. When you sent that picture, I wanted to be sick, not because of your cock, but the fact there was so much flab. My God how big is your stomach, how much do you weigh? You don't look fat in your photos, you shattered my illusion, such beautiful brown eyes, really cute attractive face, but the rest, no wonder you prefer doggy style. It's obvious it's the only way you could get near enough to a woman's vagina to stick your cock in, is that way you prefer anal sex, the only way you can get a good fuck?

This is such a let-down, like being hit in the face with a wet fish. I really was sexually attracted to you until now.

 **15:09**

Oh Luca, I'm sorry, just trying to get a reaction from you even if it's a negative reaction. I don't care how overweight you are, I'm just the same we are destined to Make Love together, I will have you just accept the inevitable, will you really deny me your cock? Oh, Luca your angry I understand that I have two weeks, then this spider will chase you and trap you in her web. Maybe you think I'm not enough for you, we will see I will have you just because I can.

147

15:41

Oh, look I'm trying so hard to forget you, but you are in my head I am crazy for you.

 **17:53**

Oh, look what do I have to do to get an answer? You're loving this aren't you, you have me exactly where you want me, I am gagging for your cock, but you will never let me near it. Maybe I should wave the white flag and admit defeat. But I really wanted to be lovers with you.

 **18:32**

You've got to want this woman, and not just any woman but the daughter of a Godfather. I hate you for doing this to me playing your little game. That damn cute face of yours those beautiful captivating eyes.

 **23:09**

Nothing I say gets an answer, you are really mad at me, this is not just one of your periodic moods. I do hope you get to meet me in Corleone. goodnight my dream lover. Not being at the end of your cock. still a woman can dream, please don't hate me Luca, let's mend the break put it back together we are meant to be its fate our combined destiny.

18/11/2021.

 10:25

Good morning, I will not disturb you I have to Face the mayor's wrath The town is becoming hostile towards me of course I can understand why. But I am pretty scared especially since I no longer have mafia protection as I had in 86.

 **21:37**

Goodnight, Luca.
22:08

 I was going to video call you but decided not to, I didn't want to make you even angrier. Plus, the fact that you would not have answered so there didn't seem to be much point.

I got all melodramatic in my next message, but I knew it was an empty gesture. But I was not going to just lay down and die, I would show him how much it meant to me to have him in my life.

19/ 11/ 2021

 **09:47**

Goodbye then the lover that never was.

11:33

Oh Luca, come on if it was really over you would have un-friended me/ blocked me. But you know how much I want you, so the game continues. boy by now your ego must be so big it's wonder you can get your T-shirt on in the morning.

 21:21

I miss your two-word messages the emoji replies. I trust you are taking good care of my sheep.

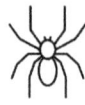 **24:13**

Goodnight, Luca my precious shepherd, I am so envious of the woman who shares your bed. I so wish it was me.

 **20/ 11/ 2021**
11:37

I admire your resolve. It's a sunny day, does your Facebook harem also tell you how sexy you are?

 **22:45**

Just reread your message on how you gave me a test, how do I know that you won though? Will you go tell your friends; Liggio's daughter showed you her vagina with confidence. it works both ways Luca.

11:38

Okay Luca, I guess I'm going to accept this time it really is over, no more messages such a shame after 26 years without sex I would have been so primed and tight as you said. We could have had amazing sex together, but I blew it. The spider is dead, the web destroyed the fly lives to fight another day.

 17:42

The continued silence says I am right, you who can be so demanding with that fat gut of yours. Prince Charming you are not. In the end I honoured my word, I was disappointed your cock was not as glorious as I had expected it would be. But still good enough for me to enjoy. Just block me, but you won't, and you know I will not do it, because I crave your body so much, what a sad cow I really am.

 **18:16**

Oh, come on, please Luca, can we not start over? I miss you so much, we've been so close. I know I am a fool, please let's meet for a drink at least if nothing else I won't embarrass you by throwing myself at you, well not straight away. chill Luca that was a joke.

I've been really stupid, I was once a very well-respected woman by some, I thought we had a deep friendship I really do care about you. it seems to me that you have been hurt in the past, and that's why you would trust no one accept yourself. you are a wonderful man, I want it to be intimate with you, was that so wrong?

I couldn't believe it, I must have touched a raw nerve because I actually got a reply, after all those messages something had pricked his conscience.

 **What do we have to start over? You talk about respect, you talk about this, you talk about that, as if you were the best person in the world.**
Then?

21/ 11/ 2021

 19:11

I am sorry I hurt you, offended you, I just wanted you to Make Love to me, I know now I am repulsive to you.

 22:47

Giovanni said I should leave you alone, but you never really cared about me, so I guess I should do what he says. I'm desperate to see you in Corleone.

Goodnight, Luca.

Is it wrong to find yourself physically and sexually attracted to someone. it is after all human nature, and if you want to get all religious about it. Is it not true that God made us this way!!!!

22/11/ 2021

 10:34

Good morning ex-lover?

 10:57

I'll try not to text now; but you can just ignore them. I really am sorry I screwed up; sorry I sent that awful photo yesterday. At least once you thought my breasts were beautiful but remember when you used to complain because I hadn't shown you them. In those days you worked wonders for my ego. Until you block me, I will never give up.

 16:01

My last goodbye, I admitted to myself that you won't Make Love to me some one might, but I really wanted it to be you. please ignore my unpleasant vitriolic comments, don't put yourself down. You really are a wonderful man.

23/ 11/2021
17:20

Just so you know, I was never joking at your expense, I was not encouraged to do this to make fun of you. the algorithms on Facebook sent me your Facebook profile as a possible friend. that is how I came to contact you. I have sent you an image of the cover of the book so you can see it really exists.

23:01

Goodnight, Luca Oliveri. I'm so excited about the book, I miss my sheep, and my wonderful shepherd.

24/ 11/ 2021

 **06:05**

Congratulations on your book.

 Thank you, dear friend, so Luca because you put my favourite picture of you on your profile how can I forget you now, did you do that to excite me.

25/11/2021.
06:31

 **Good morning.**

As Luca had responded to me after days of un- answered messages. I decided to try and entice the fly back towards my web. Using a bit of reverse psychology. It was a risk, but I had nothing to lose at the moment we were not exactly on the best of terms, so if it did all go belly up, I would have lost nothing.

 **09:58.**

Just to let you know an old flame has shown an interest

in me, so when I get to Palermo who knows what might happen. if I'm going to be messaging him it means you'll be happy to know you will be rid of my rants. take care of the sheep then I'm sure you will

 **What do you mean?**

 10:19

I wanted to Make Love with you, but you don't want to, that seems pretty obvious now. The mafioso still has an interest, I need to get rid of this sexual frustration. I wanted it so badly thought it was with you after all this time. Never mind but surely, we can still be friends, after all not everybody on Facebook is in a sexual relationship.

 **10:19**

But I can give you my little cock.

My subterfuge had worked, inspired reaction in Luca. I think he suddenly realised that maybe he had gone too far with the silence towards me and saw me actually going away from him. so, he was quick to respond. it would seem the spider was about to ensnare the fly.

Oh Luca, your cock is beautiful size doesn't matter, it's what you do with it. I thought you had turned me down; I am yours if you want me?

 **Ok.**

 Is it a yes Luca are you saying you really want me? Because I really want you just in case you haven't noticed by now.

 **13:25**
Oh Luca, we will share such passion together. I will do my best to please you, so you want me again and again.

 **Yes**
I will fuck you!!!!!!

 Oh Luca, I can't wait to be next to you.

 **when will you come?**

 15:04
Send me a picture where I can see you all in one piece.
obviously naked.

I was despondent, we had just started to communicate
again and already he was pressurising me into sending
nude photos, it was as if he was saying yes, I will fuck you.

but in the meantime, he was wanting pictures he could jerk over. I decided to give him the silent treatment for a change.

 **15:06**

OK you're gone, thank goodness for that, that I should trust you.

 **16:25**

So, you are ditching me? Last week you were done with me, then you are taking me to bed, it just doesn't make sense. Then you get all Moody because I say I've changed my mind, then you kicked me in the teeth because I haven't sent a photograph. So, we're back to the no trust again. we go round and round in circles you don't want to see me naked it's not a pretty sight. You talk about trust; You told me you were going to fuck with me. You the last of Corleone's Great lovers. tell me do you have a lot of English women who want to bed you?

I write to you.
you're online not even reading my messages!
Because you don't want to send me the photo.
I told you I'll fuck you as soon as you come to Corleone.
and you don't even answer.
Okay.

🕷 Did I not just send a message, you forget I have to translate first.

I haven't sent pictures because I'm overweight and ugly, I have surgery scars, you won't want to take me to bed when you've seen me naked, it's not a pretty sight.

You, you build up my hope, then you destroy me okay then go piss off, I've always felt you were a decent man, I was kidding myself and you were laughing at my expense.

Send me the pictures. I don't care about scars, even if you are overweight, I want to see all of you.

when you come if we fuck, will you have to undress, or do we do it dressed?

🕷 I have my Ravens to feed now, so I am not ignoring you okay.

Can you send the photo.

🕷 No Luca I am not some mafia Peep Show. Forget it someone in Sicily will take me to bed just for the thrill of having a mafiosa.

 **I don't know English right in Italian otherwise I don't understand.**

I was so mad with his hot and cold attitude, that not thinking I had written to him in English forgetting that sort of actions only annoyed and angered him. I guess it was probably down to frustration because he didn't know what I actually said. It would appear he was too lazy to translate always expected me to do it.

 **18:04**

Oh, Luca it's like an ever-decreasing circle, in a previous message you said you were glad I was gone that it was OK even said goodbye.

 **So, you don't want to fuck me anymore.**

 For God's sake man will you listen to yourself, I'm beginning to wonder if you ever read my messages or is the translation so mixed up that you're in a constant state of confusion. I am crazy about you, but you're the one that blows hot and cold. I just don't know what to think anymore, sometimes it's like I'm talking to two different people.

I said I will fuck you, and I'm not going to back

159

down I just want to see all of you.

Sorry if I have disturbed you, you seem like a very passionate man, I am glad you have changed your mind. I will give it my all. I usually orgasm several times, but then I suppose that will depend on how well you do. I will say one thing you try and fuck my arse and I will blow your cock off with a gun.

I don't understand.

You have previously said you liked it doggy style, how do I know that you won't get carried away that much you might put it in my arse and not my vagina. Being lost in the passion so to speak I guess it could be easy to get carried away and forget.

18:47

I wanted to find out if you're holding back and don't want to fuck with me anymore?

Of course, I want you to fuck me really good, but in my pussy not my arse.

That is fine.

 I arrive in Palermo on the 6th of December. I come to Corleone on the 7th.

 **I work during the day.**

 Yes of course you do looking after my sheep. God just thinking about it, it is exciting me, the thought of your cock sliding inside of me oh Luca.

 **Sure, that night, where are you staying?**

 An apartment.

 **OK I understand, you tell me the address when you get there.**

 **20:30**
Yes, it's in the town centre.

 **Boo.**

 **22:22**

What does Boo mean? I don't understand you Luca, you are a very complex man, but boy you make me want to Make Love with you more and more. I still can't believe it is actually going to happen, that after all we've been through fallouts, the insults the goodbyes, we are actually going to meet face to face. Goodnight my perspective lover. Gigliola.

 So, wish I was with you now, in your bed sitting on the end of your cock.

 **Wow.**

 That is what I want to say when we share our bodies, we will have great sex. I will kiss and stroke your cock with my tongue and lips. Now I will go to bed and dream of fucking with you all night. over and over again.

 **Goodnight.**

 Goodnight, Luca.

 **Send me the photo I asked for.**

No Luca, no photos, so we forget it! I will not be blackmailed, coerced into doing something I don't want to do because I'm so desperate for your cock.

 **You're telling me no?**

 Yes, Luca no photos, so I guess you will get Moody and won't come and fuck me after all.

 **I will give you my dick, Take it easy.**

27/ 11/ 2021.

 **05:36.**
Good morning.

11:58
Good morning lover.
12:21.
Hope the weather is better for you, woke up at three in the morning blizzards with very strong Gale force winds. I was worried about the aviaries, now the snow is almost gone, but it is raining minus 5C in the cold wind. The only thing that helps keep me warm is a thought of being naked next to you,

and us both getting all hot and steamy. I did not message yesterday I thought I would leave you alone, it's not just your cock I want Luca. I want to know you as a person too you are very special to me.

 **Thank you.**

 You're welcome.

13:21

How did it go with your book?

 It is going to be printed then goes online in a few days. Thanks for asking.

**Can I have a copy?
Or do I have to buy it.**

 I don't know until December, if it will be published in Sicily.

 **14:11**

Ok, when it comes out, I will buy it.

 14:41

You can have a free copy, but it's only in English at the moment.

 **I don't know English!**

 I am honoured you want to read it.

 **Of course, I want to read it.**

 Yes, I know that's why I will have it translated into Italian if you really want to read it. But why? To see if I really am that moron's daughter.

 I don't care whose daughter you are.

I know, but I hope someone will be interested in the book, it may well fail which means no money for the people of Corleone.

 **Understood.**

I had one of his paintings and I had no idea who sent it to me, I set it on fire along with all the documents relating to him. Hindsight is a wonderful thing, how much would it have been worth now if I still had that painting today? I hope you are having a good day and that my sheep are all fine. LOL.

I must be able to talk to you in Italian, so I can whisper sweet words in your ear, then my mouth will be too busy caressing your body my darling Sicilian lover.

Ok.
Learn Italian well for now.

21:51
Goodnight my darling lover.

Goodnight to you my darling lover.
Do you sleep naked?

Yes, so I can walk around just wearing my jewels. I live alone.

 **Right.**

 And you do you live alone; do you wear anything in bed other than your beard.

Yes.

Oh, you have excited me at the thought of your naked body next to mine. I hope this damn covid doesn't stop me travelling to Sicily, I can't wait to share passion with you.

And what will you do when you come to Corleone?

Be naked making passionate love with you, then during the day I will be at the Marilyn Cafe working on my next book.

But I want to clarify, I do not tolerate if you have other lovers that is clear!!!!!!!!

 **23:12**

Luca Oliveri, how dare you insult me what do you take me

for a common whore? I do not, nor have I ever slept around. You are a very special person to me someone who after 26 years of sexual abstinence, I wanted to share such intimate feelings with. You seem to have a low opinion of me don't take me to bed then, it's no loss to me.

28/11/2021

 **05:30**
It was just a clarification.

 **11:26**
Good morning lover.
You don't write to me today?
Have you found others who court you!

 Just a clarification, you stupid man, when I said I would be, fucking every night. I meant with you; what did you think I would do? Make my way through all the single men in Corleone. How many times do I have to tell you about how loyal I can be. until I met you, I had pined for the mafioso, I think 26 years demonstrates my loyalty to an ex-lover!

 **Did I become a former lover?**

 You insult me, then you become contrite because

168

you have blown your chance. Yes, I am gagging to be fucked. But I don't want just anyone touching me, I thought we had a connection, we fallout but we always make up. I might not be coming to Sicily after all due to covid, we might be going into another lockdown in the UK. That will let you off the hook.

 **Don't you come anymore?** **14:38.**

If you want to fuck in, May I am here.

 Luca Oliveri, of Course I want to make crazy passionate love with you. You are in my head, I want to forget all about you some mountain shepherd, but it's no good. I have spent all morning thinking about being on the end of your cock. My pussy it's starting to tingle, God man, if I can't get on that plane, I will be so mad I will explode. But be told I am possessive like you I don't like to share my lovers; you fuck anyone else, and I will blow your cock off.

 **Hurry so I can fuck you.**

16:25

So, Luca you are really desperate to fuck me? Tell me what you want to do with me please, the spiders caught her fly, now you are mine.

 **17:11**

So, you think I will fall at your feet, Sicilian men always so arrogant. I could forget you before next Tuesday.

 **Ok forget it do what you want.**

Luca are we in a mood? The man who a couple of hours ago could not wait to get me at the end of his cock. so now? Don't worry, what a shame I thought you really wanted sex with me, I feel so betrayed.

Did you say something a little bit different to normal then I react like this, if you want to come, come and let's fuck. if you don't come patience.

As you see, I am an excellent arrogant Sicilian.

 17:57

Oh, my sweet Luca, I just want to make sure you're not fooling me with your words. God, you turn me on, and you haven't even touched me yet, but believe this I'm pining for your cock.

Okay, I failed again, maybe that's forever my lost lover. But I will continue to fantasise about your cock thrusting into me, oh the pleasure the thought of it is off the Richter scale.

18:32

Oh Luca, I'm sorry I just want you, and I'm not sure if you want me really? Unless you have taken a vow of celibacy, you have to fuck someone. I'm so jealous; I want you to be mine. We don't want to be falling out when this time next week, we might be thrilled to Make Love, to fuck with such relish.

 **Sorry, but I am an arrogant Sicilian!!!!!!!**

 I don't care, just say you will still want to take me to bed. Next Tuesday evening we may find ourselves naked kissing caressing each other. I really want to kiss you with such passion, then fuck you so good you want it again and again.

I will never measure up to your civilization, as you said so eloquently well, I am one of the arrogant Sicilians, but I'm proud of that and even more proud to be Corleonese.

 Then as they say we are singing from the same hymn sheet. I was conceived in Corleone. So, I am also an arrogant Sicilian, although born in the UK. We will be fine together as we are both proud of our roots. I hate it when people say oh, you're from Italian descent, no I say with great pride Sicilian is not Italian. forgive me Luca I did not mean to insult you; you know you have power over me. Only you will decide if I get close and very personal with you, I will just leave you to decide but I am sure it is our destiny to be as one.

 **20:53**

Oh Luca, just tell me now if I've really blown it with you? Then I can get drunk on Sicilian wine of course and toast the loss of your cock. it appears I will no longer have the pleasure of.

 **21:36**

A few hours ago, you said to quote you 'hurry up so I can fuck you' I guess you've got a better offer goodnight, Luca.

29/ 11/ 2021

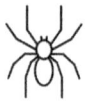 **11:12**

Good morning, Luca, so this is it okay?

 **Good morning.**

 **21:31**

Good evening. I hope you had a good day; I have been preparing for my trip, this time next week I will be in Palermo.

 **22:46**
Good evening to you.

 Goodnight lover, now only of my dreams.
30/11/ 2021.

 **13:47**
Oh Luca, you're still my would-be lover, but enough now I hope you'll be very happy alone in bed. After all I am not that desperate really.

 **14:55**
So, you're angry hence no reply to my earlier message. let me explain when I said I was not that desperate, it wasn't a reflection on you personally, I get cross when you put yourself down, your lack of self-confidence, there's nothing wrong with your penis. it's good enough for me and yes, I would have liked it inside of Me. You still have beautiful brown eyes that I totally adore. I think of you from the moment I wake up, you are a wonderful man I am lucky to have met you.

Please.

 God man, I want you so naked on a sheepskin rug

173

as you thrust him inside of me silly bitch. I always mess up.

 16:12
Luca Oliveri, damn you, you drive me crazy wanting you, I
have to get over this.

 **You'll get over it when I fuck you.**

 **16:33**
I lay in bed and squeeze my breasts and fantasise it is you,
then I close my eyes and imagine your hand sliding down my
body, sliding between my legs. If we end up naked together it
will be greater than an eruption of Etna the passion that will
be generated between us. as Kylie Minogue sang 'I can't get
you outta of my head.'

 **I'll fuck you.**

 You will fuck me, good again and again, lick my
pussy, kiss my breasts Luca?

 **Yes.**

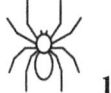 **17:29**

As I have said before I do not sleep around, I am a very demanding woman when it comes to who takes my pussy. you have caught my attention, but I think you realise that right now. I want you, promise me you will only be mine, and I swear on my life I will only ever be yours. I know once you Make Love to me you won't want anyone else. So, Sicilians are very passionate about everything they do. I think they must get it from the hot sunny joyous climate by the same token stubborn and headstrong. But they are always tremendously comic and friendly, Sicilians are always ready with a joke or a smile. to me you are that kind of person so I will forgive you your arrogance.

 **18:12**
OK.

 Oh Luca, I can't wait to be naked with you, but where? So, nobody knows about us.

 **We will see.**

 Does that mean you might fuck me after all.

175

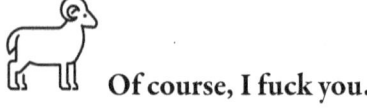 **Of course, I fuck you.**

I hope you are not offended by my intimate messages I can't hold back; You excite me so much.

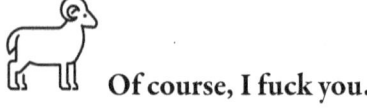 **No, I'm not offended. I will fuck you and give you, my sperm.**

I want to feel you inside of Me, the passion will consume us.

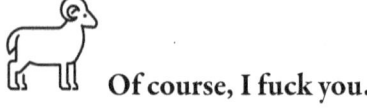 **Sure.**

I just want you inside of me, no one else just your penis, but I am not going to beg.

22:50

I go to bed alone, but you will be with me in spirit. I just have to think of you touching kissing me, my pussy starts to tingle. you have had such a profound effect upon me goodnight lover.

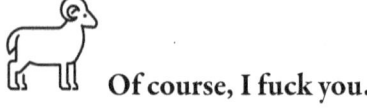 **Touch it and imagine my fingers sinking inside.**

176

Goodnight.

 Oh yes Luca, your fingers then that beautiful penis I dream of it now.

DECEMBER
01/ 12/ 2021
11:48

 Good morning, Luca, send me a picture of your face as you are now, please.

 **15:10**
No, no photographs.

 Why can't I see you? OK so your current profile is from the last two years are you worried that if I see you, I might walk away from you? After my dream last night, I doubt that.

17:02
What's with the shrug? Is it the truth really, you're just

dumping me. Yes, you've decided you don't want to fuck an old woman after all. I don't think it's me, you might have other ideas.

 **I told you I fuck you; I fuck you!!!!!**

 okay Luca calm down, chill. I didn't want to offend you, now you are angry I seem to make a habit of doing that making you angry. I just want it to be special for both of us.

 **16:28**
I will give you, my dick.

 I'll give you a good fuck Luca.

 **18:04**
Hi Luca, I hope to build that passion when we are in bed. Last night in my dream we were naked on a sheepskin rug.

 **20:47**
I have just taken a bath and now I'm lying naked on top of my red fox fur coat, fantasising that your naked body is next to me. maybe I should bring it with me when I come, then we can fuck on it Luca. you will love the feel of the fur against your penis, it's so sensual. Tell me what will you do to me Luca?

 **Send me a picture.**

 To quote you Luca, no no photographs, you will just have to use your imagination for now.

 **23:15**

Goodnight lover, I can't wait to kiss your beautiful penis.

 **And if you want only once, it will be only once. OK?**

 Goodnight

02/ 12/ 2021

 **22:00**

Did you miss me today, two days and I leave for the airport would you have me once?

 As much as you want.

 Sorry I don't understand. If it was up to me every day if you'd like that?

179

 **22:44**

I'll fuck you when you're here.

 Yes, but will it be only once?

 **As I've said before if you want it only once it will be only once.**

 Oh, Luca I will want you again and again if you want it to.

 **Ok.**

 Goodnight, Luca.

03/ 12/ 2021.

 **11:36**

Good morning, Luca, just to show you what you could be missing.

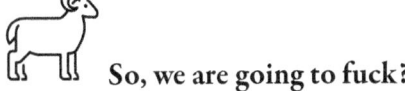 **So, we are going to fuck?**

Oh Luca, so you liked what you saw?

Yes, two great senses and a mouth to rest my cock on.

23:05
Good night, Luca.

181

05:42
Good morning.

20:35
You don't make yourself heard anymore.

I'm sorry Luca, it was a crazy day trying to get everything ready to leave tomorrow. Did you miss me?

So come to Corleone.

I will arrive in Palermo on Monday afternoon I should arrive in Corleone on Tuesday afternoon.

And we get laid?

I thought it was what I really wanted, but now I'm not sure if it will be appropriate, I suddenly feel like a whore, unpaid prostitute, begging you to take me to bed, this is not the kind of person that I really am.

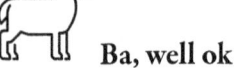

Ba, well ok.

I'm sorry Luca I'm confused, I just feel cheap and nasty, worried you will think that I am a slut.

 **No, I don't think anything.**

 Maybe when I get there and I meet you things will be different, and the feelings will just click in to place, and we will spend a passionate night together.

 **OK, given all the past speeches and those of tonight. I cannot help but say goodbye and wish you good luck.**
You bored me now.

 22:31

There it is again, that arrogance of yours. you don't seem to comprehend how I feel about this! I don't go around Facebook asking strangers to meet me in person to take me to bed. it appears to me that you were never going to do it anyway you were just making a joke at my expense, leading me up the garden path to see how far I would go. your loss Luca I would have fucked you really good.

 **You're the one making fun of me!!!!**
You enjoyed making fun of me?

183

OK you did well.
However, to be clear. I had understood. I thought you
would pull back and that is what you have done.

 No, you're wrong, it was never a joke to me being intimate with someone it's not something to joke about. thank you, you helped make my mind up. when I arrive, I will message you, you say where and when and I will meet you. we will go to my apartment; we will get naked together and then hit the sack. I will prove to you that this is no joke, that I was serious, I will give you the best ride of your life.

 05/12/2021.
00:46.
Good morning Luca is it really finished before it's even begun? We are so close now tomorrow I fly into Sicily after so many years away, it will be tinged with sadness for me but also with joy because I was going to meet you my wonderful shepherd. Now it seems that I have fallen at the final hurdle.

 08:43
If you walk away from me, you will never know if it was all just a joke. You will never know if I really did find you sexually and physically attractive. can you go on with your life not knowing the truth.

 20:14.
I know you wanted to see me as soon as I arrived in Palermo,

and it's wonderful that you would come all that way to meet a stranger. it's not that I don't want you to come, it's just that I promised Evelyn, that I would see her, her parents have separated, and this is the first Christmas that they will not be together. She sees me as her aunt even though we're not related, and I wanted to do something special for her, so I have gone a bit overboard bought her lots of presents. She has such a lovely smile I don't like to see her sad. Are you going to let a little girl Come between us for the sake of a day or two.

 21:10

video call to Luca no answer.

 21:48.

video call no answer.

 I tried to video call you, I guess the reason you didn't answer me it really is over. I notice you've changed your profile picture You know what I'd be missing? Goodnight my lost lover.

 22:15.

You would never have been serious about us getting together, so I gave you the perfect way out. yes, you leave me wanting, but you've done me a favour your ego is as big as your body.

22:38

Damn you Luca, I will not back down I will have you. I bloody well will be kissing and caressing your beautiful cock.

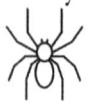 **23:43**

Goodnight sexy shepherd.

07/ 12/ 2021.

 **23:04**

So are you ready for a laugh I am not in Corleone, not even in Sicily. They would not let me on the plane, my lateral flow tests had expired. But all is fine, now flying on Friday so I will be with you Saturday afternoon. Then I guess you're not interested anymore? Did you change your profile again to get me hot and bothered, well it worked, God, I want you goodnight.

 **11:21.** Luca Oliveri, what are you doing to me? Another change of profile boy you're loving this, that I created for you the power you currently have over me. like playing games do you Luca?

 **12:57**

Oh Luca Luca, talk to me Luca, you haven't blocked me. So, you must be having second thoughts.

Luca was in one of his infamous moods nothing, it didn't matter what I seemed to say he wasn't having any of it. Of course, I was sure his ego must have trebled in size because although he was not replying he was marking that he'd read my messages, I had no idea what was going to happen. I sat in the airport lounge with little else to do, so I thought I might as well continue to bombard him hoping that at some stage he would decide to respond.

 22:04

Goodnight lover.
09/ 12/ 2021.

 **06:07**

Good morning, Luca.

 **17:23**

I will be arriving in Palermo on the 10th of December just in case you're interested.

10/12/ 2021

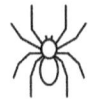 **01:52**

I'm at the airport; waiting for my flight. the fact that you haven't answered any of my messages not even with a customary two-word answer an okay or an emoji shrug of shoulders. Leave me to believe that it really is over between us before it ever began. So, I admit defeat, please take good

187

care of my sheep I wish you all the best, I hope Santa brings you true love for Christmas.

 **14:51**

Well Luca I landed this morning. You are no longer interested in me?

 **20:49.**

What do you still want?

 You naked making love to me.

 **Don't you think it's time to stop this pissing off!**

 The bath here is huge, we could have such fun bathing each other, it's even big enough so I'm sure we could fuck in it with ease.

 **If it weren't a piss take.**

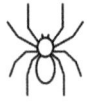 **22:50.**

Hark at you, have women lined up to get into your bed. what the daughter of a mafia Don not good enough for you.

 **24:04**

video call no answer.

11/ 12/ 2021

O5:16

Come to Palermo tomorrow night and let's get physical Luca, please.

09:19

video call no answer.

You are a liar Luca Oliveri, you just played along. otherwise, you would be here sharpish, especially after you kept going on about wanting me to hurry up and come. Words are cheap, they can be meaningless, just words. sex offered on a plate; an Englishman would have bitten my hand off.

But you don't want me to come to Palermo, because there is someone already there waiting for you at the hotel!

Oh Luca, I thought I had explained this to you, it was a friend and the little girl Evelyn, I told you about. I want you here Luca, there has never been a man here in my bed. tell me you will come tomorrow night?

When I wasn't able to get on the plane. Due to the language barrier, when I video called Salvatore to tell him that I would not now be flying until Friday he had just nodded, I thought he had understood, but I had later found out that was not the case. I had not seen his rather curt message he had sent the evening of the 6th demanding to know just where I was. Luca had now sent a screenshot of Salvatore's message. I didn't know whether to be angered or flattered, that Luca had been looking at my profile page, so he had seen the message from Salvatore, the fact that he was now reacting in such a jealous manner led me to believe, that Luca did really care about seeing me. Except from his next message, it appears I should take nothing for granted.

 **You called her friend, but I think she's a friend with a dick!!!**

 08:58

OK Luca, I lied and said it was a female friend and not a male friend, exactly for this reason that is now become apparent to me. I did not want you to think, that I was meeting Salvatore to go to bed with him. He came with his daughter, to get her Christmas presents. What did you think we were going to do make love in front of her? Yes, he is a

190

male friend, he never has nor ever will be my lover. I do not want to tarnish our friendship by becoming emotionally involved in a sexual way. My only concern is you. I have come to realise that you are not a very trusting man, there's nothing wrong with that. However sometimes you have to trust those who want to be close to you okay.

 13:57.

The fact that you haven't replied to my earlier message, I guess proves that you no longer care. but I'm not one to just give up. In fact, I'm glad you want me to fight, because it will show you that I am honest and sincere in regard my feelings towards you.

When I arrive, I will stand in the town square, and shout as loud as I can in Italian, so everyone knows what I am saying, that I want to make mad passionate love with a local shepherd called Luca Oliveri.

No reply, I've seen you read the message Luca, okay I'm crazy enough to stand there in the square and do it, as the English say, 'never dare a fool'.

 Oh, come on Luca, please.

 **But please what?**

 Let Me kiss and caress your beautiful naked body, share your cock with me Luca.

 **Didn't you like your friends' cock?**

 Oh Luca, I have never seen, nor ever had the benefit of Salvatore's cock, as I have already said I never want to, I only want you. damn it man.

 You don't understand shit.

 Me, now you are joking me, the one that won't understand, that there is nothing between Salvatore and I, or any other man. how many times do I have to say it, it's you, you, you, you.

 **Take his,
if you want that.**

 Mamma Mia, when I come to Corleone on Monday, I will find you, I will demand that you come to my bed, and we will Make Love. As a lady of honour, you can be sure of that.

 Come now Luca, come to the hotel and spend the night with me.

 **Of course, I should be second to him.**
I am second to no one!!!!!

 **15:12.**

Oh, oh Luca, why won't you listen, you are second to no one. I did not ask Salvatore, who did not turn me down. You can be so infuriating at times. he is not, never has been, never will be my LOVER, I am hoping that will, be you?

 **15:34.**

It would have been so beautiful when my tongue licked your genitals. licking and then sucking your cock, so as you once said you came in my mouth gave me your sperm as a gift. I've only ever wanted you Luca.

room 214, the Ibis president hotel via Francesco Crispi, opposite the entrance to the port. sex all night Luca are you not just a little bit tempted?

 **One can't for dinner.**

 You are going out tonight, so you won't bring your cock down to Palermo, can't we Make Love until you're

exhausted, begging me to stop.

 **OK.**

 Does that mean you will Luca?

 17:39

Will you see me yes, I know Luca.

 **20:00**

Oh, Luca I've just had a thought, your cock, it's not Caput is it.

 **If you write in English, I will not answer you anymore.**

 I said you wouldn't fuck me, because your cock is caput. Then that's not a problem, just means lots of foreplay fingers can be just as exciting.

 **OK, then I'll put it up your arse and let's see if it is caput!!!!**

194

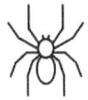 I knew you would come back with a rebuttal; Now you will have to come tomorrow to prove to me that it isn't.

 **You will come to Corleone, right?**
I'll wait here.

 **21:42.**
I will arrive on Monday, returning to Palermo on Saturday, so we will see won't we. but I'm telling you now, there is no way you are shoving it up my arse.

12/ 12/ 2021

 **17:50.**
Palermo is a beautiful city, but I can't wait to return to Corleone, I want to meet you so much. I had a wonderful dream of you last night. then this morning. I really like you, but you might not have been vaccinated against covid.

 18:38
No, I didn't get the vaccine.

 So, you have the perfect excuse to back out, to not have sex with me. I wonder what you would say as an

195

excuse if I said I didn't care if you're vaccinated or not?

 **No excuse, I didn't get the vaccine.**

 Good, then there won't be any problem with us getting up close and personal.

 **I have no problems; in fact, I haven't asked you if you've had the vaccine. if I did come to the hotel, you would have to find out if I could come in without the green pass.**

 I can always come to your bed Luca.

 **when you come to Sicily yes.**

 Have some of my messages not got through? I am here in Palermo. I'm getting the bus to Corleone at 12:00 o'clock on Monday. due to arrive apparently at about 2:30. so that gives me ample time to find my apartment and settle in, while you are out in the field looking after my sheep.

 **And when do we fuck?**

 Wow Luca, you're suddenly very keen. as soon as you like Monday evening my prospective lover.

Tomorrow night then?
And give me the address tomorrow.

20:59

Indeed, I will Luca, I'm already getting excited. Tonight, I will lay in this massive bed, and you will consume my thoughts.

OK

13/ 12/ 2021

07:06

Good morning my darling shepherd, I'm so excited, I shall miss the huge bath, and have to make do with a shower. but the sacrifice will be worth it, knowing I will be naked next to you. At long last able to gaze into those beautiful brown eyes that I am so captivated by. The address is Casa Chiaro di Luna diesa 9 Corleone. sorry obviously.

 Ok, are you already there?

 No, still at the hotel in Palermo, have breakfast book out and go to the coach station. I am so excited, it's crazy. cannot believe after 26 years, I'm also a little apprehensive how I will be welcomed. There will be no meeting the mayor hugs and kisses. Maybe there will be a few of the older people who will recall that day in August 86.

 **Ok.**
Are you coming alone, or do you have company?

 08:39

What do you take me for, I'm unmarried, no engagement ring on my finger I travel alone.

 **I didn't mean married or engaged?**
I just asked if you were travelling alone or have company.

 I travel alone, no mafiosi in tow. No one will know I am a Godfather's daughter, unless I choose to tell them. So, no one will know your dirty little secret, now we are going to sleep together.

 **OK.**

 God I'm going crazy here; well, you know where to find me. it's up to you whether you come or not.

 **I'll come.**

 08:58

OK.

 **16:39.**
You arrived?

 Yes, and I am waiting for your body.

 **I come after.**

 After what Luca?

You're not going to come are you?

 **Of course, I come. First, I go home, then take a shower and eat and then I come down, but I will still lose a few hours.**

 Ok, when you get here ring the buzzer and the door will open automatically.

 **I'll tell you when I come.**

 Now Luca then we can Make Love all night.

 **Yes.**

 **20:10**
Are you there?
Ok, not even read the message it means you don't care.

 where are you?

 **I do not understand.**

Sorry are you coming or not?

 **Yes 5 minutes you'll be at the door?**

 Ok.

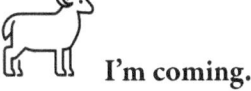 **I'm coming.**

Via diesa Oddo right
I am here.
you open, open the door.

I opened the door standing at the top of the marble staircase just my black satin dressing gown on, I watched in awe as he closed the door and came upstairs as he reached me, I open my dressing gown to reveal I was naked. He just said wow, flung his arms around me and we kissed with such passion I had never kissed like that in 26 years. It was a long French kiss; I remember momentarily thinking about covid. But then I didn't care there was so much passion in that kiss. It was as if we were long time lovers not two people who were just meeting for the first time. I was so excited as I led him to the bedroom, he was well built like me overweight, but I didn't care, I just wanted him. To feel his shepherd's hands on my body, to feel his lips kissing my breasts that he so adored.

We had both promised so much in the end it didn't live up to expectations. He was like a little boy lost there was no more passion, that kiss had been a one off. We talked to a fashion, he told me how old he was and how many sheep he had with the aid of sign language. The bed didn't help, I hadn't checked before I booked the apartment that the bedroom had a double bed, it hadn't. there were two small beds fitted into this tiny room we tried to make the most of it. it was impossible for us to lie side by side. At one stage I got cramp he was a true gentleman and massaged my leg until it went, then I got my leg stuck between the mattress and the wall it was more like a comedy film.

I feel mean saying this, but I have to be honest, he was right about his small penis, it was like a miniature chipolata. But I wasn't going to kick him in the teeth and spent most of my time trying to give him some self-worth, he seemed very depreciating of himself, as if someone had been, really vicious and vitriolic towards him. It was strange but I wasn't bothered about the sex, although that's what we'd originally met for. But he seemed a kind gentleman and even though we couldn't communicate with the language barrier, we had chemistry, there was a connection between us, we seem so good together. I no longer just saw him as some Sicilian to fuck. He was not a sex god like the mafioso of 86/ 94 but this man needed someone to care for him, to care about him. he noticed my Ferrari watch and said he also had one. we bonded; we became as one. when it was time for him to leave, he got to the bottom of the stairs turned round and blew me a kiss that was a beautiful romantic gesture I had not expected then he was gone.

I was shell shocked, unsure what had actually happened, to the Passion he talked about, the oral sex the foreplay, the wild unbridled sex. I was unsure if I wanted to go through this frustration again, he just laid there, it was almost as if he didn't really want to be there, maybe he was gay, but wouldn't admit it to himself. Maybe he had just been nervous I know I was and had not exactly been a sexual goddess, I couldn't get Valerio out my mind, I felt even after 26 years I was about to betray him. that one kiss, he never tried to kiss me again, never said my name. I spent more time looking at my watch, wondering if it was time he went, knowing because of his job he would have to be up early, it had been a complete disaster. one I was not in a hurry to repeat.

23:59

As soon as Luca got home, he must have got his watch he sent me a photograph of it, he said the only reason he hadn't worn it was because it needed a new battery. I did not reply to his message instead I sat at the kitchen table a glass of wine in my hand and tried to make sense of the last three hours. He had caressed and kissed my breasts, we did had intercourse, but it was bland like food that had no seasoning even though we had the obvious connection. Did I want to see him again? After 26 years without the touch of a man on my naked skin, I went to bed more frustrated than I had been before Luca touched me it had been like trying to Make Love to a corpse. So, I had to decide what I was going to do, was I going to be honest and tell him the truth I was unsure how to proceed. Should I not at least give him another chance? I decided that I would be sensitive to his feelings, he did seem like a man that had been repeatedly hit over the head with a big stick, who had been mocked either by his peers, or maybe a previous lover. I was going to be his fairy godmother, hiding behind the arrogance I was sure he was a very kind and sincere man. I was going to help to try and restore his self-esteem, so I was basically going to lie to him, but it was with the best intentions at heart.

14/12/2021

06:15
Good morning.

Good morning. thank you for last night, I am glad after all the name calling, the fallouts, the goodbyes, that at last, we came together and how beautiful it was to be naked next to you. when I was sat astride you, and you held my hands, gave that beautiful smile, and I was at last able to gaze into those gorgeous brown eyes it was wonderful.

Thank you.

Will we meet up again or am I delusional.

09:28
when you want.

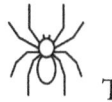 Tomorrow night lover?

 **Wednesday**

 **Wednesday?**

 Yes please, tomorrow night.

 11:25

Have I asked you if I can see you on Wedensday?

 Yes, I will see you tomorrow and I will already be naked.

 **Wow.**

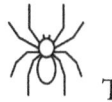 Well, why waste precious time undressing, I want to undress you, nibble your ear, who cares if you've got a hairy chest, to be honest last night I never really thought about it. It was just so beautiful to see your naked body.

 **Really.**

205

 Yes, Luca have a good day.

 20:28.

My dear Luca, all I've thought about all day is what happened last night, tomorrow I am sure it will be even better.

 **Sure. what do you do today??**

15/ 12/ 2021.

 **08:39.**

Good morning, my lover, sorry I did not reply to your message last night. I went to the Excelsior bar, by the time I got home, I had to charge my phone.

16:30

 Are you coming tonight my sexy shepherd.

 **Yes.**

 18:13

I can't wait I need you to come now and please me. Please hurry.

 **Later.**

 If you can't spare the time, maybe we should forget it.

 **18:43.**
I do not understand.
Maybe you don't want to see me anymore?
Let me know if I must come or not.

 **20:09**

Come tonight when you are ready, I was just starting to wonder if you would come or not.

 **If you don't want to see me, you can say it.**

 Oh, my darling Luca, of course I want you to come now. Or is it you that does not want to see me anymore?

 **If you change the subject every 5 minutes, what am I supposed to think?**

Are you going to come or not. I've been a disappointment to you I'm sorry Luca.

**5 minutes and I'm with you.
I am here.**

This time we were both more relaxed he was still trying to put his finger up my bum but did not force the issue and when I said no, he was a true gentleman accepted my decision. He like I prefered to Make Love doggy style, so I was elated when he asked me to kneel up on the edge of the bed, he bent over me and entered from behind, it was so beautiful him thrusting into me. I was so glad that I changed my mind and decided to see him again. The only problem I had as he got more excited and thrust even more forcefully into me, my knees were starting to slide on the sheet of the bed and the momentum was pushing me further onto the mattress, this meant my feet started to lift off the floor until I was on my tip toes and eventually because of this lost my balance and collapsed onto the bed. But it had been so beautiful, I couldn't wait to do it again. I was falling for this guy in a big way he had such a wonderful smile, he appeared to be so kind and gentle, and I was sure he didn't just see me as someone to have sex with.

While Christmas shopping, I had noticed some wooden decorations shaped like Christmas trees, they had names on, so I bought one that had Luca's name on. I had meant to give it to him on Monday but had forgotten. I had written a love letter for him, so wrapped the decoration in the love letter, and that evening when he came, I slipped it into his body warmer. He must have read it when he left once back at his car because within five minutes, he had sent me a message.

 **Thanks for the nice words you wrote to me you are a very special person.**

23:10.
Are you there?

Yes, my lover, thank you that was a lovely thing you said to me, a thought I shall treasure and hold precious for the rest of my life. Goodnight and once again thank you from the bottom of my heart.

Goodnight.

16/ 12/ 20 21

08:02
Good morning.

 **10:47.**
How long are you in Corleone?

209

 We will see each other one last time tonight.

 **12:45**

Sorry I did not answer your message before, but I have been to the cemetery to put carnations On my grandfathers and father's tome. I started to cry after all he was my father apparently. tonight, will be our last night together, that's if you're coming?

 **Of course, I'm coming it will be sad to have to say goodbye.**

 **13:32.**

Yes, we have spent such a wonderful time together, tonight I will kiss and caress your beautiful penis hold your naked body close to me one last time.

 **See you tonight.**

 **14:17**
Sì.

17:36.

19:16
If you want, I come?

 Yes yes, I am waiting for you.

 **Ok, I arrive in 5 minutes.**

 Thank you, my darling.

We had a wonderful evening, he brought me two gifts a big box of panettone something I had never had before, along with a bottle of Don Corleone liqueur. I guess a nod to my

211

presumed father a true don of Corleone. I was worried I
might not be able to take the liqueur home with me I wasn't
sure about customs, Luca was so sweet, he was desperate
for me to have it He even said I should give him my address
and he would send it to me. I told him that was a very kind
gesture, but UK Postal Service would only allow bottles of
a certain size to travel through private mail, so it would
probably be confiscated once it reached the UK. He looked
genuinely gutted. I didn't want to let him down so I said
I would sneak it into my suitcase, as I thought if it was in
the hold of the plane, it probably wouldn't be a problem, we
had a selfie taken together, then undressed and made love,
I didn't want to leave him he was so sweet and gentle, we
really had bonded. It was so hard saying goodbye. Little
did I know what would transpire a few months later.

 **23:00**

**I know I've already told you this the other day when you
gave me that lovely love letter, but you are truly a very
special person, and I am glad that we got to meet in the
end and shared some wonderful moments together.**

Oh, Luca you're the special one. I don't want to
leave you, but I have to go. but we can still message each
other, and I have that selfie of us together, you look great me
I look quite hideous. I will keep that picture at the side of
my bed, I might also have one on my desk, so you are always
close to me. I know you will take good care of my sheep, and
I hope that next may when I come again, we will once more
be naked together. goodnight my sweet Luca.

17/ 12/ 2021

 **06:00**
Good morning.

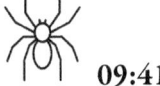 **09:41**

The naked mafioso just something to remind you of me. I cried this morning; I don't want to leave you or Sicily. take care my sweet, sweet Luca. my darling lover

213

 If you don't take care of my sheep, there will be trouble, don't be sitting, down and texting me, but I like it when you do Luca thank you.

My beautiful, shepherd.

Yes.

21:00.

Oh Luca, I am so alone without you. I am already starting to miss your tender touch, cuddling you so we are as one. Goodnight my love.

21:41

So now I have left Corleone, will you be fucking someone else now Luca Oliveri?

 **22:02**

Have a good return home.

18/ 12/ 20

06:30

 Oh, my dearest Luca, I am so sorry I was vitriolic last night. I was in a bad mood but that's no excuse. I had a terrible argument with the bus driver before I left Corleone. he was not going to let me on the bus he would not accept my green pass to start with. Until one of the students who spoke English explained to him it was an NHS approved document and gave me access to travel on public transport throughout Sicily. I so enjoyed so much last night, I hope we can share the passion again next year when you can come to

Palermo and share this beautiful big bed with me.

 **07:20**
Are you at home or still on the go?

 **08:16**

No Luca, I am still here in Sicily, back in my hotel room until Monday afternoon. I miss your beautiful smile and those captivating brown eyes. you are a marvellous man the women of Corleone must be crazy not to try and snap you up. then I think like me, you're a person who prefers his own company of just your dog, and my sheep.

 **Thanks.**

 You are starting to put distance between us OK Luca I won't bother you again; all the hearts and kisses are all bullshit.

 **But it's not true.**
So, I come and see you tomorrow night?

 What, you would come to Palermo, tomorrow say

goodbye before I go home. Really oh Luca that would be wonderful, the bed here is huge we can have so much fun in it, after that stupid little bed at the apartment. do you mean it will you come?

 **If you want.**

 Want, of course I want you to, to be close to you one more time for our bodies to be entwined as one. Oh yes please say you will come; you will come Luca.

 **10:03**

Give me the address in the morning I will come tomorrow evening.

 **10:47**

It is the Ibis president hotel 230 via Francesco Crispi. Don't worry about the green pass as long as you bring a mask you will be fine; I want you in that bath first, that is just something else I have never seen a bath so big; it takes an eternity to fill. Once we have bathed together then we will make passionate love one more time before we say a final goodbye.

 **Yes.**

I couldn't believe it, he really wanted to come all that way to Palermo to spend the night with me. I felt bad now that

217

I had assumed his tokens of affection were just for show, when in fact he had given them to me with true feelings of affection, it would be even harder to get on that plane on Monday morning.

 17:44

You will really come tomorrow?

 OK

 **Yes,
After work in the evening.**

 **19:04
Ok.
What are you doing.**

 Sorry Luca I was lazing in the huge bath thinking of you in it washing your back if you really do come.

19/ 12/ 2021.

 **05:12
Good morning.**

 Good morning my lover.

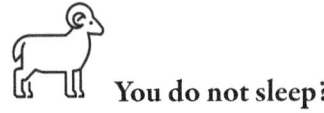 **You do not sleep?**

I had a bad night, really bad tummy ache, you don't have to come if you don't want to? it is a long way to drive.

 **Come.**

I am glad that you will, you will love the huge bed all this space I want our last night to be very special.

05:49
Yes.

08:14

I tried to video call, but this Android phone is rubbish I need to get an apple like my daughter has.

219

 Thank you, lover.

 **You're welcome**.

 17:44

Come.

 Sorry I mean come later; promise me you will come.

Yes.
The address again.

 Hotel ibis presidente 230 via Francesco Crispi, okay.

 **Ok.**

 I can't wait, I'm so excited, wound up like a spring.

18:21
But is it in front of the port?
Ok I will wash take the car.

 Yes at the opposite end of the port where passenger ferries dock.

 **I do not understand.**

 Just let me know just before you arrive, and I will see you at the door.

221

 **Ok.**

 Thank you, lover.

 **20:09.**
I am in front of the door, but I don't know if I can leave
the car here.
You are there?

 I am here, there is a parking lot behind the hotel.

 **I am here...**
I wait for you to come down.
I am already in front of the door.

I went down to meet him he managed to park the car
at the opposite side of the road just across from the
entrance to the port. I was naked under my Indian dress
which I had worn purposely, once we were in my room.
I turned to face him unzipped my front opening dress

*and let it fall to the floor. He just said wow. I went and
lay on the bed gyrating while he undressed, spreading
my arms across the bed telling him we had all this space
to indulge our sexual passion. Once he was naked, he
joined me on the bed it was such a beautiful night. I
had expected that he would go, the night was made all
that special by him staying. It was wonderful just lying
there watching him sleep. I was falling head over heels
in love with this man, but I knew deep in my heart that
it couldn't be, he lived here in Sicily, I lived hundreds
of miles away in the UK. Not only that but there was
the age difference, which did not matter to me, but it
might to him. we had made love, we had talked using
the tablet as the translator it had been so magical, he
was so excited to learn about my life back at home in
the UK, I remember him saying scribe scribe, so he could
understand in Italian what I was trying to tell him.
morning came he got up to use the bathroom, there was
no more sexual contact between us, in fact very little
was said. He got dressed as did I, he had to remind me
to put my mask on and we walked down to the front
door together. I remember the receptionist giving me a
disapproving look as we exited the lift. Once outside he
gave me a hug, we didn't kiss. I stayed and watched him
walking across to where he parked the car, he opened
his car door and then looked across obviously to see if I
was still there. when he saw I was he waved blew me a
kiss and got in his car and was gone. I waited expecting
him to drive past the front of the hotel, but he must have
gone around the roundabout taking a different road.
Once back in my room I lay on his side of the bed and
cried into the pillar he had slept on, I could still smell
his beautiful body scent.*

20/ 12/ 2021

 **06:15**

 **06:59**

My dearest Luca thank you for making my last night in Sicily so special. I will miss you desperately, but next spring will arrive soon, and I hope covid allowing I will be able to return to Corleone. my dear lover Luca Oliveri.

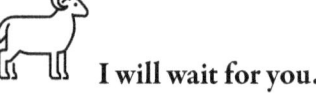 **I will wait for you.**

 Oh Luca, thank you for that thought, so beautiful made me cry tears of joy. I love you so much.

 **23:14**

I have got home OK Luca.

21/ 12/ 2021

06:07

Good morning.

 Good morning my darling.

 **Are you at home yet?**

 Yes.

 **Everything is good.**

 Yes. Except I am not there, and you are not here.

 **Ok.**

21/ 12/2021

 08:18.

Arrived in London okay my darling.

 **09:31**

Sorry Luca about the brief replies, I was travelling on the bus so no access to the Internet. I am now back at my own house. I was so sad yesterday as soon as the plane took off, I cried, I was so upset that the passenger next to me asked me if I was OK. I said I was just sad that I was leaving someone who was very special to me as well as leaving Sicily. I didn't really turn you on did I, I got all frigid, try to lay the blame at your door in my head. but it wasn't your fault it was me. It meant so much to me that you stayed the night, it could have been that it was because you just fell asleep, but I don't care, I won't think of it like that, I will believe you stayed because you wanted to be close to me, after all you told me on different occasions that I was truly a very special person.

Don't worry, I was just tired because I'd had a hard day. I know I let you down, I am sorry, then falling asleep.

Oh, my dear Luca, I know you work very hard for long hours looking after my sheep. I just wanted to please you to thrill you, God I miss your beautiful smile your hands on my breasts, please you will say we will make love again Luca?

226

 **Of course.**

 **17:01.**

Do you have a girlfriend in Corleone? please tell me if you have one, I don't want to share you with anyone else, I just want your beautiful body for myself. I am a snake who will coil around your body, I will consume you with my passion.

 I just want you to be close to me, it can't be though, I must leave you I must let go.

 **I do not understand.**

 You are a younger man Luca; I am an older woman you need someone who loves you of your own age. I am in love with you, it broke my heart to leave Sicily yesterday leaving you there. Thank you for the magical time you gave me, thank you until we meet again goodbye my darling Luca.

227

 **When you want to come to me, it will only be beautiful.**

 You are such a wonderful man; you are not making it easy for me.

 **19:00**.

I have great feelings for you, if I could come back to Sicily on the next flight. I thought it would just be sex, but you have captured my heart, I am yours only as long as you want me to be. My Don Corleone arrived intact. so, I've just had a drink to toast you my lover.

 Thank you, my panettone not so lucky, it now looks like a squashed loaf of bread.

 **Patience.**

Be patient about what? Giovanni is already on my case, he is saying I am letting lust cloud my judgement, that eventually I will cry be sad and alone.

 **Understood.**

Is Giovanni, right? That you will drop me if I get too intense, if you do, do it now before I come back. Then I can go through the grieving process, I know that when I come next may. I will not be seeing you.

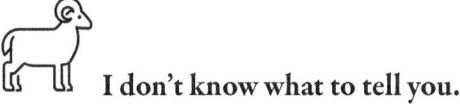 **I don't know who this Giovanni is, and I don't even want to know it anyway, you see what you want to do.**

I want to love you, Giovanni still thinks he can control me, but my father has been dead 27 years I never wanted it to happen, but it did and I feel lost in the dark, not knowing which way to go. Tell me Luca what do you want?

I don't know what to tell you.

**You should think with your own head and not with someone else's head.
Only this I can tell you.**

 You said you would wait for me; I think you are an honest sincere man, I want to be part of your life, we have shared so much together in such a short time, please Luca be mine. Gigliola.

 **I will wait for you!**

 **20:20.**

Oh Luca, thank you. I am yours for as long as you want me, I love you.

 **20:13**

I remember so well that Monday, when we first met, you came up the stairs and kissed me with such passion, you never did that again, in fact you never kissed me.

 **When you come back I will.**

230

I know it will come because I will consume you with my passion.

Goodnight my lover, I miss you already and it's only been a day.

Goodnight.

Trying to catch up on some sleep was travelling all night. Don Corleone is powerful stuff just like you.

Look I'm really crazy about you is that okay?

 **Wow.**

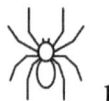 I said this truthfully, no bullshit. I keep looking at your photos on Facebook, I love that mean and Moody look you have some of them, it makes you very attractive. I'll sleep now and think of next year; you and I back in that big bed.

 **Yes.**

22/ 12/ 2021.

 12:05.

You see I have a problem,
A real serious problem.
I miss you Luca, oh luca how I miss you.
Loving someone so much, I love you.
Needing and wanting someone as much as I want you,
I cry when I am not with you,
How much I miss you, you are constantly on my mind.
I am crazy about you; never leave I couldn't live without you.

 **12:11.**

12:26.

Over and over, I look into your eyes your beautiful brown eyes.
you are all I wish for; you have captured me.
I want to hold you, I want to be close to you, I never want to let go.
I wish that kiss had never ended, and then I could have had that kiss forever.

 **12:43.**
It was wonderful.

 14:40.

Oh Luca, you are a very special man. I loved every minute of being close to you, but sadly I had to leave you, because my time in Sicily had come to an end. You are there, I am here, you have really got to me I am falling hopelessly in love with you, but it can't be true, I'm such a romantic fool. I can't stop thinking about you. I'm sorry I didn't want to complicate your life, I'm sure I have in a way that you were perhaps not prepared for. Then I may be presumed too much, and that you feel as I do.

15:04.

 You shouldn't encourage me, but I love your kisses. Especially when I hope to personally receive them, I so wish I was there now to kiss you.

 **We are far away now.**

 Yes, you will forget me now. I shouldn't love you Luca.

**15:59.
If you want to forget me?**

 They say love is a magical thing. I would say that will keep you away from pain. I would promise you my whole life, I have never been close in all these years, to a wonderful man such as you. I thought you would be the one to stop my tears, I am scared so scared, I love you, but I have lost you. I'm going to be alone confused again no, no Luca I love you, and I will fight to the death for you, I thought you

234

wanted to forget me.

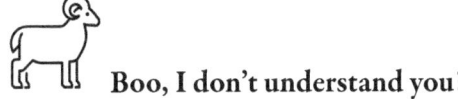 **Boo, I don't understand you?**

   I don't understand you, you, you lie, what is
there to understand when you said we are so far away
now. I thought that was your way of saying goodbye, but I
misunderstood, did I? I'm crazy about you, you know that
I've cried because I don't want to lose you, I never thought
it would be a problem, you would have sex with me. I never
realise that I would fall in love with you, but I did, and I
want you to learn to love me, we were destined to find each
other. The romantic reflections I am very sorry, but I want
you to know so much how precious you are to me. This is
not nor has ever been a game for me, it might have been for
you.

 **17:37.**

Yes, I wait for you.

   Okay my dearest Luca, now I've cried because I am
happy, I really do love you. I thought you wanted to finish it,
I am happy that you are still mine, will you always be mine, I
hope all my sheep are well and of course Vaso?

235

 18:42.

Ever since Luca had made the comment about him being so far away. Now the little voice in the back of my head was starting to throw doubt on his sincerity. Then maybe I was doing him an injustice, it could be that he was experiencing emotions he was not sure how to deal with. I was in danger of alienating him with this thought process, I had to tread carefully.

 20:46.

After you said we were so far away, I decided to do something about that, so I've been looking for Properties for Sale in Corleone. For a little house maybe that I could renovate. I hope you don't think I'm getting carried away, but I just want to be close to you; to see if maybe we have a future together? I'm drinking wine and I dream of seeing you next spring. Goodnight my lover.

 Goodnight .

 21:43.

A quick question am I not really sexually attractive to you. I ask you because on the 5th of October, you said in a message that to quote you 'you have to do the foreplay, and then the unbridled sex'. But nothing like that happened, you only fingered me when I put your hand there and it was not the kind of fingering, I was used to. I was very let down by that? In your messages you sounded so passionate when you talked about sex, but I never really saw that passion did I? Be honest with me Luca was I really such a turn off, I know I didn't exactly set the bed on fire myself; I should have done more to get you excited, but I couldn't get the mafioso out of my head to start with. but I thought we got there in the end, didn't we?

23/ 12/ 2021.

 07:50.

My Lover Luca.

Please Luca answer me.

09:37.
Good morning, Luca.

 **10:14.**

I would take the stars out of the sky for you,
Stop the rain from falling if you ask me to.
I would do anything for you, your wish is my command,
Words cannot express how much you mean to me.
You are the sweetest song I can sing.

Do you not want me to love you Luca? Well, I do, and I always will. I will fight to the death for you. Please don't turn your back on me what have I said to upset you, it's like old times before we met in Sicily.

Thank you, my dear Luca.

 11:22.

Oh Luca, I think I understand why you aren't answering my messages. Sunday night was wonderful when I felt you slip inside me and we were as one it was magical, we were both nervous, you had a hard day taking care of my sheep ha-ha. you've never asked me why I call them my sheep? Not everything is about sex, I don't just see you as a piece of meat to maul in bed. You will become a doubting Thomas again, doubting that I am sincere and honest, I'm sure you're back to believing that this is a game, but have I not proven myself to you, you make me laugh, you have a wonderful smile, you are a truly lovely man and I want to get to know you so much.

15:03.

Tell me what you want me to be?
There was that kiss and boom you were the only one for me.
I'll be whatever you want me to be, you make me, roll me
control me, console me, thrill me delight me.
Because of this I am crazy for you, please be mine Luca.

Or is it over between us?

 15:21.

'I'll be waiting for you'. Is what you said, you arsehole!!!!!!
now I'm back in the UK, its old news, you screwed me,
proved you were a man and now you throw me out with your
trash. Are you enjoying knowing you broke my heart, what
was it I've always said about you? Kind and sincere, almost,
that is the laugh of the year.

 15:42.

So, the word is goodbye,

it makes no difference how the tears are cried, it's over,

and my heart lives alone, I can make believe you need me
when it's over.

I can't take it home, that fire that was burning inside of my
heart for you.

Gotta give some of the love inside, don't take it away and
watch me die.

239

I made sure I loved you and we both played along together, but now for some reason I don't understand, it's all over, and I cry alone in my heart ache.

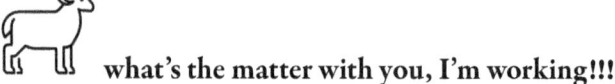 **what's the matter with you, I'm working!!!!**

 You did not say good morning, I thought it was your way of telling me to get lost that's all, maybe these pathetic love messages were driving you crazy, I'm sorry if I have got it wrong. I just thought you might enjoy a little romance as you drive along in your tractor or herding my sheep.

I was pushing the boundaries, becoming too intense. why did I suddenly doubt him? Had he not told me on two separate occasions that he would wait for me. Did he not send romantic gestures? I was in danger of pressing the self-destruct button, if I wasn't careful, I would lose him. But even though that little voice in my head was once again telling me to rein myself in, I carried on the same path ignored that little voice. like my friend Giovanni had said it would all end in tears.

16:05.

I miss you so much and I'm worried, being as you once said so far away, I'm worried I will lose you to a beautiful lady in Corleone. I'm sorry I should be more trusting I'm really crazy about you, I just hope we share the passion once again very soon. I can't get enough of you Luca you have consumed me. I think in reality you are the spider, I am trapped in your web, but I do not complain because it is heaven. I'm just afraid of losing you I know you are sincere; it was wrong of me to call you names I am so sorry it just wasn't necessary I should trust you.

 **I told you I will wait for you, and I will wait for you!!!!!**

 Thank you, Luca. I'm sorry I don't mean to be so intense I just miss you so much, it's only been two days what will I be like when it's been two months?

19:08

 **20:18.**

Look I'm sorry I'm a Moody cow today. I'm also sorry I was intense with those romantic words. I will leave you alone, I'm just insecure, that there is someone in Corleone having your cock, When I have claimed he is mine. Thank you for the kiss, I will treasure it goodnight my dear ex-lover.

 **Goodnight**

20:52.

I shouldn't want you, but I can't help it you look so sexy in your profile picture complete with mafia shades I have that picture in a frame.

 **Which Foto?**

 Profile picture you're angry, yes?

 **We see.**

 **23:02.**

Is it wrong to have a picture of you, the one on my phone is not good, you look great. But me I look like the bride of Frankenstein; if you are cross I would do better not to send you any messages.

24/ 12/ 2021.

 **12:26.**

God Luca Oliveri, I miss your cock.

242

I often miss you; do you miss me? Merry Christmas see you in May.

🐏 **13:34.**
Merry Christmas.

🕷 **16:29.**

Luca, Luca?

🕷 **16:54.**

By the time I see you again, I will be so sexually frustrated for you, it will take two days to recover. We will share such wild unbridled passion what do you say? I would sit on your cock all day if it was possible. God man what have you done to me.

Luca sent a gif Christmas tree.

🕷 Beautiful, thank you my sexy shepherd, I am trying to leave you alone, but that exquisite piece of equipment you have between your legs has like your eyes captivated me.

243

 I can't wait to feel your lips on my body again.

 Don't go away from me will you, we have so much passion to share Luca it will be so beautiful. Sofia and I are starting to crack open the Don Corleone, when I am dancing around the office to some music.

 **17:45.**
who is Sofia?

 Sophia is one of my Ravens, boy Luca just to give you the heads up in case you hear about talk around town. I had problems at the guest house, so when I did my review, they were offended because I told the truth about

the problems I had with the electricity. Now they are saying to my daughter, that I as Liggio's daughter asked them for protection money, which is quite funny if it wasn't so serious, I am only connected to the mafia, because there is a possibility that murderous lunatic could have been my biological father. Don't believe all this rubbish about the lace, it's really not true. But I suppose in a way it's all good publicity for the book it will bring it to people's attention goodnight sexy shepherd.

 Goodnight and Merry Christmas.

 **Goodnight and Merry Christmas to you.**

Thank you.

You're welcome. Is the marketing of your book going well? You could get me a gift for my next birthday.

I know I can get you the battery for your Ferrari watch, how about a new tractor with all this protection money I will have.

I was kidding, I won't be able to ask for gifts.

why not?

 Oh Luca of course I'll give you a present. I never thought I should have brought you some cigars from duty free. I only realised yesterday what type do you smoke? Now I'm going to take a bath two things I miss most all about Sicily, is your wonderful body and that huge bath.

25/ 12/ 2021.

10:15.

Two identical Christmas trees with a Red Bow sent by Luca.

Thank you I was lying in bed thinking about you then my phone pinged it was you wishing me a Merry Christmas. A kiss for you and your beautiful dog Vaso.

I miss you my sexy shepherd.
I still think you are the spider, and I am the fly consume me Luca with your passion.

11:56.

I decided to video call Luca, just to see him wish him Merry Christmas to his face, I let it ring then chickened out and hung up, I had a wonderful surprise when Luca rang me back, he looked great had a black woollen hat on he gave me such a beautiful smile blowing lots of kisses at me and then he was gone. But that was the best Christmas present I could have received; I was still to the front of his mind, and it was good to know I had not just been a quick jump because it had been thrown in his face. It appears I had meant something to him after all where will this lead us? Will we fall deeply in love; should that happen would he want to marry me? Of course, I was getting ahead of myself I'd only been home for a few days, so it was all still fresh in both our minds how did I know it had not been some kind of holiday romance? Would the distance in the end prove too much of a challenge, only time would tell.

12:14.

It was wonderful to see you, you look sexy in your woollen hat, well you look sexy without it, it was so magical to see your beautiful smile. The guest house now thinks I'm going to set fire to the apartment, Is everyone in Corleone crazy? Well, I will be the talk of the town. My daughters told me there terrified it really does beggar belief. I suppose I should be flattered that there are some that believe that what I am saying is true. I'm not sure if I should be a little bit apprehensive about this? I don't want the British police coming knocking on the door accusing me of mafia association.

 **Booo.**

Luca had the habit of using words I did not understand, they must be Sicilian as they would not translate into English. at times it was quite frustrating because it meant I didn't fully understand what it was he was saying to me.

 I don't understand my lover, I know you must be sick of hearing me say it, but it was so wonderful to see that beautiful smile.

 **13:28**

248

15:09.

Oh Luca, thanks for the kiss, it makes me feel all warm inside. I really can't wait to see you again, to share your body with mine, I love you so much my sexy shepherd.

15:38.

 **16:16.**

You are so romantic, nothing like the Luca I used to make angry. I just want to say again that I really appreciated you coming all the way to Palermo to see me on the Sunday night, it was a lovely gesture.

16:36.
So, you are a mafioso?

He came out with his question completely out of the blue. I tried to ring him but there was no answer plus the fact that once I had put my brain into gear, I realised there wasn't much point, I didn't speak Italian and Luca didn't speak English. But I had to make him understand I was not now nor ever had I been a mafiosa. I decided the best thing to do was to message him, this was not the kind of Christmas present I had wanted to wake up to find out that I was part of the mafia Organisation.

I am not a Mafiosa Luca, it is simply not true the people that own that apartment are making it up I'm sure to tarnish my reputation. All this because I gave a negative review on booking.com but I did state that there were good things about the apartment that I had found very good. Being such a fussy eater, it was great there was an oven and a cooker, so I could prepare food to suit my own particular pallet. I am sure this is a smear campaign to damage sales of the book, which is a negative attitude to take since sales of the book are to help the people of Corleone. I'm disappointed though that you will believe them first rather than me? We have been so intimate together, I guess it was just a quick jump after all. I guess this means we are finished to be honest I had a feeling for a few days now that you were looking for a way out well, they gifted you the perfect excuse.

Please Luca, it's not true I am not associated in anyway with the mafia, over then the possibility that Liggio Was my real father. Please Luca do not let the Mafia destroy what we had. it's like Valerio all over again, I lost him because of the damn Mafia. I am crying now I am so distraught about all this, that people in the town believe this of me.

even you don't believe me, why are you doing this to me? How can you turn your back on me like this when you said I was such a truly special person to you.

**Ok.
I believe you.**

250

my mother's death bed confession, is still ruining my life from beyond the grave, she wanted revenge for whatever reason; my God she's getting her money's worth.

Please Luca.

Thank you, thank you Luca for believing me.

20:42

 Goodnight.

Thank you, I felt I was going to lose you because of a stupid comment on a website, that has little to do with you and I.

26/ 12/ 2021

 **04:55.**

I cannot sleep good morning my sexy shepherd have a good day. it might be Christmas, but the livestock still need to be seen to wish my sheep are happy Christmas from me.

 **Have a good day.**

 **16:49**

Hi dude hope you have had a good day. I translated my book into Italian, drinking a glass of beer amoretti, we'll have a couple of shots of Don Corleone later. God, I miss you, it will be so hard when I do have to say goodbye, but I know in reality this will happen sooner or later.

I want to wrap my body around yours like a snake and consume you with wild intense passion. Tell me what you want me to do, to turn you on, to please you Luca. To see you in ecstasy because you were bathed in my sea of passion..

Hello.
So, did you drink today?

I was confused by this comment, I know I called him dude, which was a bit unusual, but was he suggesting I had a drink problem, it was Christmas after all. so, I had a couple of bottles of beer, and was going to have couple of glasses of liqueur did that make me into a raging alcoholic? I was perplexed I could not wait to read his explanation.

 Yes, I've had a little drink, to ease the pain of losing you. I have started to stare reality in the face, you are a younger man I am an old woman well not that old, I have to let you go, you need to find someone more around your own age.

 **Maybe you drank too much.**

 You condescending bastard. I'm as sober as a judge, you really kicked me in the teeth. you're the one that makes it seem like I fucked up. Have you made a lot of women cry Luca? Because you made me cry, does it make you feel good, then block me if you don't want me to love you.

 **But what happened to you tonight?**

18:20.

Damn it man I'm madly in love with you, but I can't expect you to love me. I know if I come in May, I'll have to say hello, when I came to Sicily, I just wanted a Sicilian cock inside of me, to relive the night I had with the mafioso. But it was more than that with you, just to be close to you. I didn't know I was going to fall in love with you, but I did. it scares me that I'll have to let you go, because I don't want to, I'm not sorry Luca, I will never regret being in love with you. But I have to be realistic about this if I was 10/ 20 years younger, then I would leave the UK and come to Sicily, but I have too many responsibilities here. I have grown up children, grandchildren. then there are the Ravens, my vocation at the castle the Queens Raven keeper. I cannot give all that up on a whim, because I think I'm in love with you, I want to spend the rest of my life with you. At the end of the day, it could just be a deep infatuation. And I have to take into consideration, that is all it is as far as you're concerned, you may not be looking for a deep meaningful long-term relationship. So now I am going to get drunk yes Luca, drink myself into oblivion and mourn my lost love.

[Luca mark this message with a crying emoji.

 **I expect you the same.**

 I am going to say what you so often say I don't understand what you mean, you expect the same for me.

254

 **Yes.**

 I will not just give in; we can have an open relationship that would be one way to go. I will not give you up without a fight, there must be some way to get around this, the casual relationship when I come to Sicily. Maybe you might find that more appealing? I am not asking you put a ring on my finger Luca, just that you will let me be part of your life even if it's just over messenger. I won't cry anymore.

20:15.

My dearest Luca, what must you think of me, it's been a long day all this business with the mafia, then I should have known to expect something like this, but after 37 years I really didn't think anybody would care. But that's no excuse for being so vitriolic and taking my frustration out on you, let me love you, you don't have to reciprocate. In the end the only one that's going to feel pain will be me. Let me live the dream just a while longer, after all this time at last the mafioso has gone; you make me happy let me live the dream for now at least. You are giving me the strength to move on.

 **Ok.**

 You forgive me then; I know it wasn't just a quick
jump for you. you wouldn't have travelled all that way
to Palermo, when I'm sure there's someone in Corleone
that maybe sometimes shares your bed. you felt it too that
connection, the chemistry between us that was very real to
both of us.

 Are you mad at me like you used to be in the old
days, I know I'm a silly old fool, goodnight my darling.

 **Goodnight.**

 Will I get a kiss tomorrow?

 **Ok.**

 Answer yes or no you have to be totally honest do you want me to write to you?

 **Yes.**

27/ 12/ 2021.

 04:29.

As you can see, by the fact that I'm sending this now, I have been unable to sleep. I don't really know what's happened to us since Christmas Day, but things are not good between us, are they? but I can at least say good morning.

 **05:15.**
Good morning.

Thank you, Luca.

 **10:26**
Your welcome.

I now know why I was such a moody cow yesterday, I have the most excruciating toothache, the side of my face is so swollen, it's quite scary. It is cold and foggy here a typical December day. I am also in danger of losing the most precious thing, I have found in years, you. I will be loyal will never betray you, even when you tell me to go away, my love for you will never falter.

 I know I sound like a broken record that you are sick of listening too. Please let me love you, you are such a wonderful man, that emoji has made me feel so much better, I am happier now, considering my toothache gets more painful by the minute.

 **12:48.**

Excuse me sexy shepherd, should you not be out looking after my sheep? Not chatting on your mobile. Have a good day, after some painkillers earlier, my tooth does not seem so bad now.

 **Yes, but I am working, you have a good day.**

 Of course, I know you're working, I was just kidding you, I am glad we appear to be friends again. I know I have acted in an appalling manner towards you, I am so sorry. Now I do some work, it might be holiday time for some, but like you I have work to be done.

Although we had appeared to be back on course especially with the kiss Luca have sent me, I still wasn't sure. I think now I was back at home; he had gone back into the groove he was in before we had met. I was sure things were sliding downhill from Luca's point of view. I was trying to convince myself, without much success, that it had after all been nothing more than a holiday romance, now it was time to get real. Maybe although he would never be such a cad and admit it to me, it had just been a bit of fun for him, sex without the trimmings, you know no dates, no hearts and flowers, no promises of undying love, why would he turn it down. I had to derail this train, at this particular moment in time, I had no idea how I was going to achieve that, and even if deep down it was not what I really wanted to do anyway.

 **17:21.**

I cannot deny the deep sexual attraction I have for you.
I think looking back now, that it wasn't what you really
wanted. That first night, I don't know maybe neither of us
knew what to expect. I know it was anal sex you wanted,
how many times did you try and put your finger up my bum.
Giving me that beautiful smile, trying to get me to submit.

 Yes, you know I like anal sex.

 That is very true, maybe in the end that will be
the straw that breaks the donkey's back. Or whatever the
saying is. Someone would say, that in a relationship you need
to learn to compromise, but which one decides what that
should be.

 **17:53.**

Thank you for the kiss sexy shepherd.

 **19:06.
Your, welcome.**

 **20:00.**

Luca, I had a long think while I was having a bath, I have never had anal sex, so how do I know if I'm not going to enjoy it. Little steps Luca, you will need to be gentle with me, not going like a bull in a China shop, maybe a wrong expression to use. But if it means that I please you, hear you groaning with ecstasy, as you thrust inside of me, then I am sure it is worth the sacrifice.

This time I will submit willingly, no need to smack my arse to distract me. I have read that it can be painful, if you don't use lubrication, especially as the muscles will want to push against it. Not only that but in the bible such action is forbidden by God. The fact you wear a crucifix around your neck, means you are a hypocrite and a sodomite. As the song says, 'The things we do for love.'

 **So, I will have your arse?**

 Yes Luca.

 **Perfect.**

261

Promise you will be gentle, start slowly?

 Of course.

 **20:37.**

I hope you will like my arse. Will you dream about it Luca? Goodnight

 **Buonanotte.**

 **21:35.**

I have read some more about anal sex, so I think I am ready. I hope you appreciate this, what I am ready to do for you?

28/12/2021.

 **04:46.**

Of course, I appreciate it.

 **05:15.**

Good morning my love.

 **Good morning**.

 **09:33.**

Work, work.

10:22.
English humour sorry.

 **Ok.**

Put your cock up my arse. Especially after what happened in Palermo, we have never really talked about that, have we. Have a good day, I have only another 210 pages to translate into Italian, wish me luck.

 14:19.

I have been on a woman's forum, they say men prefer anal sex, because they are secretly gay, it would explain why you were not turned on by me.

 15:17.

Now I have committed to anal sex, does that mean you think you can ignore me? Or are you just really busy. Or have I offended you, it will not be the first time I doubt it will be the last. Look if you were gay, you would not have gone off on one about Salvatore at the hotel. Me and my Liggio mouth, yet again I did not engage my brain, before I opened my mouth. Before you tell me to go fuck myself, yes, I should. Looks like I won't be fucking you in the arse or anywhere else come to that.

 17:50.

I will not give up on you. We have come so far in a couple of months. It was those stupid articles on the internet, they put silly ideas in my head. You adore my breasts, if you were gay, you would not give a toss about them. Forgive me, let's try anal sex together you and I, it could be really good, so satisfying for us both.

Video call no answer.

This was the beginning of the end, although at the time I did not realise it. I never meant to insult or hurt Luca, when I made a comment, he might be gay because he liked anal sex. the fact that he was not replying to my messages left me in no doubt that he was really mad, and I knew all too well that when he was like this, he would switch off from me. I Had this stupid idea to get him to talk to me. Boy was I about to light a fire that was not going to be so easy to extinguish, if at all!

Please Luca, I am really sorry. OK Luca I will post on your Facebook page; I will tell everyone we were lovers in Corleone and I am madly in love with you.

Do not dare.

You see I knew that would wake you up forgive me remember Luca; you should never dare a fool.

I will block you, and as a result you will have lost me forever.

No, do you think that I would do that? I only said that because I was desperately trying to get you to talk to me. I know how much you guard your privacy. Please Luca don't leave me now, what we have is beautiful, just see me once more in May, if you're not going to see me what would be the point of coming? I could just promote the book in Palermo.

Video call no answer.

 But you will see me next may?

Luca replies with a kick in the teeth.

 **I don't know.**

Those three little words were not what I wanted to hear. This was a dagger in the heart, I was so sure that because I agreed I would let him have my arse. he would be more

266

than willing to see me, that had been my ace card, but I've never been much of a poker player; I had been outplayed by Luca. I got all soppy and emotional, something that would only anger him even more.

 No Luca, please Luca, you know I love you why does it have to end like this? This is what you wanted and now I've given you the excuse, you should have blocked me like you said you would, what is happened to that kind gentleman I knew three weeks ago? When I came back from Sicily, the emoji lips, twice you said you would wait for me. Even got really cross with me when I doubted your word, how soon you forget. Now it seems it was all just a huge lie, is it because I've fallen in love with you? But you are a free spirit and do not want to be tied down. I guess my arse it's not worth fucking after all.

 **19:58.**

Audio call no reply.

Please Luca.

 **20:26.**

Yesterday you were thrilled I said I was going to let you have anal sex with me. I got nervous, I searched online about it, listened to bad advice, and now because of that it's all gone wrong. You phoned me on Christmas Day, you blew me kisses, but I never meant anything to you really. God man I didn't want you to put a ring on my finger I've told you that before. I just wanted to be near you, to share my body with you, I know you are very angry with me, it has been a long time since we argued, I want to look into those beautiful brown eyes again, now I leave you alone. I will have one or two glasses of Don Corleone. goodnight my sexy shepherd.

 **20:33.**

Video call no response.

 **21:16.**

I will always love you Luca, even if you drive me out into the desert, I will come again, the accommodation is booked complete with double bed, but it seems I no longer need it.

 **22:03.**

Video call please Luca.

 **22:17.**

Video call no answer.

 OK you have broken me; I will go back to the sewer that's where mafiosi belong I'm just another rat.

29/ 12/ 2021.

 06:33.

Mi dispiace Luca per favore.

Non mi piace il modo in cui ti comporti con me.

 what you wanted me to do was a big problem for me okay! I was wrong to react the way I did; my tooth is still causing me problems. In Palermo with you it was so magical, please Luca I need you I plan to spend all night with you. I just wanted to please you; I did a great job didn't I? Please Luca when I really want your beautiful cock in my arse. now, I will never have it, how ironical is that; have a good day.

 **Have a good day.**

 I agree to the one thing that will make you happy and I end up losing you, how does that work?

10:01.

Forgive me Luca, I would never humiliate you I know you are a reserved man; I respect you I just wanted to talk to you I was wrong I'm a stupid fool, please Luca don't leave me yet, not so angry with me, you can't deny what we had was beautiful wasn't it. You gave me back my self-esteem you made me feel like a woman again, gave me the push I needed to move on to forget the mafioso, to get on with my life. I will always be grateful to you for that. Now I will do what the English always do at times like this have some tea and work, I will miss you, even the sky is crying.

 Did you kill the spider???????

 12:28.

It has stopped raining here, but it is still raining in my heart.

Oh, Luca I still have terrible toothache now I have heartache, my toothache can be cured my heart can only be mended by you. I am also sorrier than I can ever say. I never meant to imply that you were gay, it was a stupid thing to say I am trying to work, but the image of us together hurts my heart.

 15:32

I've just finished another chapter. I was going to send a

picture of my backside, but I decided against it as you are already mad with me, so it was not perhaps one of my better ideas. Please don't block me Luca I can't stand this; you're leaving me alone despite clinging to a single silk thread until maybe? Could you forgive me, I didn't want to hurt you, I just want to love you, just for a while please Luca look at what we had, what we had was very special, we laughed together we made love together we even went to sleep together. I don't think you're a heartless man.

 15:38.

At the moment you're just a very angry man, and you have every right to be.

 **16:52.**

Luca to get rid of that anger, you will have to put your beautiful cock up my arse. With that unbridled passion you told me you had, like when you slapped my bottom, you can't make me enthusiastic and then say I can't have it. This is just bad Luca, especially now when I want him so badly.

 **17:25.**

OK Mr Oliveri I surrender I have lost you forever even if you have not blocked me, thank you for letting me have the pleasure of your beautiful body.

Just know that no one will touch me ever again. I will always be yours, maybe one day we will at least be friends, if not lovers once more.

 18:45

Good evening, Luca, my sexy shepherd. I have been drinking my Don Corleone, when you gave me that I meant something to you. it has helped cure my toothache.

 21:37.

Do you have someone else? My fault if you have, goodnight my sexy shepherd, I have killed what we had now, I will get drunk and then fall asleep.

Not the way I wanted to end the year. No matter how many messages, video calls I made there was no response, in an act of desperation I asked my friend Ernest to help me.

30/ 12/ 2021.

 09:17.

Luca please, please Luca. Ok, goodbye then, but know one thing I love you so very much.

10:27.

what does your friend want with me!

Of course, I could not let Luca know I had set him up so he would message me, I got Ernest to tell Luca how desperately sad I was, how I was crying and drinking and not eating and that if he just messaged me occasionally, all right it would give me false hope, but it would prevent me from getting very depressed and who knows maybe suicidal.

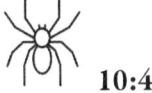 **10:45.**

Sorry Luca my friend, I have no idea what you are talking about?
I will kill him what did he say? I'm so sorry, I had no idea, he would get in touch with you. It has just made things worse for me, you are less likely to forgive me now. Will we never be friends again Luca?

I don't want Salvatore, I never have. I just want you to be my friend or cut me off completely I am so sad.

I work now on my book.

I sent verbal messages, but all went unanswered, New Year's Day came I wished him all the best of course being polite he wished me the same. I sent further messages, tried to video call but nothing one brief message he replied to with his customary okay. I had threatened to write on his Facebook page that I was in love with him.

JANUARY

01/ 01/2022.
10:57.

 **Say hello to them all for me.**
Goodbye.

As I told you, since you write on my Facebook page, I
block you.
Goodbye.

 **11:30.**

I didn't want to luca, I love you, but you are killing me. You
will not accept my apologies, you don't care about me, all
I do is cry I can't sleep I can't eat; I only drink myself into
oblivion. It was my only line of defence to hurt you, like
you are hurting me now, I tried to remove it as soon as I had
sent it, but it was too late you had already blocked me. I will
always love you and your beautiful penis, I was just being
vindictive because I know how sensitive, you are about your
penis, please forgive me I do love you. Let us not start the
new year in anger.

He had at least allowed me to reply before he had pressed
the block button, I have been very vitriolic and deeply
regretted the course of action that I had taken but it was
too late. I had written on his Facebook page that we had

met through Facebook, and arranged that when I came to Corleone, we would become lovers. But it had been a disaster, because he was about as passionate as a corpse and his manhood was laughable. I would admit that at times I can be spiteful, but had I stopped to think first I would have realised that yes, these comments would really hurt Luca, but more importantly the spitefulness might have garnished a response from him, but it had killed any future relationship even friendship stone dead. now I had to try my best to attempt to salvage any chance of reconciliation. maybe on this part it had been a spur of the moment thing because for some reason he suddenly unblocked me. I wondered was it because of the message from Ernest, or did he have feelings for me that he had suddenly come to realise? Whatever the reason I had some very serious grovelling to do.

 12:44.

Thank you for unblocking me. I'm such a stupid bitch at times, I just want to love you, be a friend, maybe a sometimes lover, I want you so much, for you to show me the passion of anal sex, at the moment I am now at peace. I will not bother you, because I know you are very angry with me, you know where to find me if you want me as a friend. In the meantime, look after my sheep.

I will just be polite and only say good morning and goodnight, so I still feel close to you.

 **14:09.**

I know I said not so long ago I would only say good morning and goodnight and here I am messaging you in the middle of the day. This is madness, will you never forgive me? What happened to us, on Christmas Day we were so close, now we are worse than we have ever been, you even laugh at me, I guess it is no less than I deserve. Did you unblock me because deep down you really do have feelings for me or is it just so you can twist the knife you have stabbed into my heart. To me you always seemed a kind sincere man, it would seem I got that very wrong, pathetic Gigliola, I guess I must be to love a man who was so mean to me, the arrogance of yours treating me with such contempt.

 **No, I will never forgive you, for posting on my page.**
you should not have written that post.

At times Luca could be so infuriating. if he was never going to forgive me, why had he unblocked me was this his way of extracting revenge? Have me on a string, let me message him bleating on, while I boosted his arrogant Sicilian ego he so loved to brag about.

 Block me, tell the stupid bitch to go fuck herself, but you won't will you? Because of your oversized ego, because you love the fact I'm here crying and moping over a bastard like you.

 **14:41**.

You just wanted to crush me, well you have, laugh at me, laugh at me again, you talk of your pain! What about the anguish you have caused me in the last few days, behaving like a spoilt child. All that supposed love, the kisses. I reacted the only way I knew, pissed off, because of some damn shepherd who wrapped me around his little finger, did it make you feel good Luca? Treating me like sheep shit on your boot. You should be a Mafioso, liar, a hypocrite, definitely not the honest sincere man I thought you were, more the fool me.

You wouldn't talk to me, and I didn't know what else to do. I never meant to hurt you, I regretted it, but I was severely pissed off, because I love you, but you'd left me long before I ever published that. I just did not realise that until now you must have loved it a man, who referred to himself as ugly. Suddenly there is a woman almost begging him to make mad passionate love with her, at the end of it all turned out to be a crap lover, and that is you not me!

 **You knew that by posting such despicable things on my page, that I would block you. I told you I would, and I did.**

We are not getting anywhere, you said it was what you

wanted, so we did, four times. But it was not how I imagined it would be. You talked a good fuck, that was about all. I just want the pain to end, I'm in such a mess. Why don't you believe me when I say I love you? This is the first time in days we have spoken and sadly it is all in anger.

 **Yes, because I'm too angry with you.**

Okay I accept that, so why not do it then? Tell me to fuck off, block me and for good this time, then you will never need to be mad again, unless it is with someone else, who piss'es you off.

Now I get drunk, lament my loss with a glass or three of the liquor you gave me, thank you for that, it was given with sincerity. Just know this Luca Oliveri I will always love you and I will never betray you. I will remember with fondness the wonderful time we spent together.

 **15:37.**

You shouldn't have published that post.

You said if I posted on your Facebook page I would lose you forever, but in reality, I had already lost you the moment I got on that plane.

 **But you posted all the same**.

 I was drunk, I did it on my laptop always forgetting not to press the enter button unless I was really sure I wanted to send the message.

 **However, you did it was on your page.**

 Yes, but I never meant to send it. I've told you; I was in a bad mood drunk; it was a mistake. I was so cross with myself because I knew what might happen, maybe in hindsight that was what I wanted, you to be so angry you would block me. Was I just a quick fuck? It was offered you thought it would be impolite to refuse.

Tell me if that was the case, then I can hate you pretend I never liked you that my suppose love for you was just a whim. That will be so easy for you. Maybe you want me to fight for you, so you can see I mean it, when I say I love you?

I have had time to reflect, I was not exactly on fire in bed, was I? I did not try to stimulate you, excite you. I could have started the foreplay, but all I wanted was to get your cock inside of Me, at the time nothing else mattered. All I could think about really was my last mafioso I wanted you to please me like he had. Expecting you to be like him and take the lead. I did not give you the attention you deserved; I will always be sorry for that. I used to refer to myself as a spider it would appear you have stamped on the spider, and she is now dead.

If it really is true that you will never forgive me, put your arrogance to one side and kick me out of your life for good!

 17:26.

After the wonderful time we shared now, all there is the darkness that we now know.
on these regrets I have grown accustomed to.
it was my responsibility, and you gave me nothing.
you never could have it all, we were destined to hit a wall.
I know now that my tears will have to dry on their own.
so, we are history, your shorter shadow caresses me as I stand alone.
only love, but I had for you comforts me, as my tears dry on their own.
I wish I could say without regret, without emotion, dude I thought we would never get to kiss goodbye.
But the sun will still set, the moon will still shine, the rain will still fall my tears will have to dry on their own.
now it is just me, and the love but I have known, as I stand here all alone.

 Goodnight.

 Fuck your goodnight.

Well, for someone who was trying to get back in Luca's good books, swearing at him was not the way to go especially as

he was saying goodnight to me. But I was angry with him, and I knew his good night was him just being as ever polite, he didn't really mean it. I so wanted him to block me, but he was not done with me yet, all I did was constantly feed his arrogant ego. I had come to see a side of this man that I really did not find appealing.

I now saw him as a useless lover, who was grossly overweight, had about two teeth was going bald, was bad tempered and Moody I could go on, but for all his faults, I was in love with him, so it was not that easy to say goodbye. I remember when I had a deep infatuation for Gianni the police inspector. Giovanni had advised me the best way to forget him and break the infatuation, was to make a list of all the negative points to Giannis character. I was trying to do this now with Luca, but it was no good because this wasn't just an infatuation, I was deeply in love with this man. I'd known from the first meeting that he was the man I wanted to spend what little of my life I had left. But that had just been wishful thinking on my part I had to break the chain that bound my heart to him.

02/ 01/ 2022.

05:19
Good morning.

08:37

Good morning.

I tried desperately not to text, I can't help it if I'm in love with you, I know I will never be forgiven. I can't stand this.

03/ 01/ 2022.

 **05:29**
Good morning.

 **05:54**

Good morning.

I sent numerous messages, but all went unanswered, so I sent the selfie we had taken at my apartment there was no message, but he had put a thumbs up on the right of the photo.

 **21:28.**

Goodnight Luca

.

04/ 01/ 2022.
07:05

I was annoyed because the next day he had said good morning, even though I had not said it first with this in mind were things starting to look up. Maybe his anger was at last starting to subside, but I had to be mindful that this might not really be the case and he was just being polite, but at least it meant I was to the front of his mind, as he went about his daily work.

Good morning, Luca, I hope you have a good day.

05/ 01/ 2022.

 05:29

Good morning my sexy shepherd.

 **10:10**

 10:25.

why do you send me a photo I have already seen!!!!

 Oh, I'm sorry I didn't realise I will send a different photo.

Remembering how he'd once being annoyed that I hadn't sent him a naked photo of my breasts, I decided foolishly in an effort to win him round I would send such a photograph now. I was devastated by his retort, and I realised that this ship had well and truly sailed.

 Don't you feel cold like that?

I will never feel cold while I have you to keep me warm.

I sent numerous messages throughout the day, but all went unanswered I even tried to video call, but it made no difference. I was getting more and more annoyed, why didn't he just block me, why when he blocked me before did he then unblock me. So, we were back in the loop was he playing a cruel game at my expense?

I was now starting to see just how arrogant he really was! Could I really love a man like this? Would I be able to cope with his bad temper, his moodiness. I couldn't stand arrogant men, I remember his chauvinistic attitude when I was able to tell him what breed of sheep he had, he had shot me down saying he was sure I was a man, because I was too clever to be a woman. Gianni displayed the same arrogance, maybe it's a common trait maybe all Sicilian men are arrogant, maybe Sicilian women just have to learn to live with it.

20:04.

 Goodnight my sexy shepherd.

 **Goodnight.**

06/ 01/ 2022.

 **00:45.**
Good morning.

06:17.

 Good morning, Mr Oliveri.

For once it was I who was stunned, but also confused. I was not going to get too excieted but taking into account the time he had said it, maybe for once it was, he who drank too much.

 **10:12.**

I want you, to please you, in the end it would seem the big breasts aren't enough. So, I guess we have nothing more to talk about it is very difficult to find out, that you are as exciting as a wet fish. Take care Luca, you will always have a special place in my heart, of course I'll be madly jealous of the bitch who shares your bed now. It's what I always wanted, you. But if she makes you happy when I couldn't that will make me happy. I know that you will take care of my sheep and that beautiful dog which now I will never be able to meet.

 **11:04.**

I told you do not comment on my page, and you did it heavily!

 **11:47.**

I fell madly in love with you, but I knew it couldn't be. I am in the UK you are in Sicily, I had to make you hate me, I knew what was going to happen, it seemed like the only way to get you out of my life, be angry enough to get in touch with me but other than that it doesn't explain why you was so cold to me in bed? There was no real passion, other than the first kiss at the top of the stairs. I thought we were going to have one hell of a night; I also knew the bed was against us a passion killer being so small. Why the hell did you have to send me a message, oh Luca, I only did it so you would hate me, you said you would block me, and I would lose you forever. But here you are, even though you haven't forgiven me and say you never will, you are still in my life, in the end sex didn't matter to me. I will always remember you saying scribe scribe when I was trying to tell you about my life in England about the Ravens, the castle. Do you remember how we both laughed when I came back from the bathroom and trumped, we laughed in unison. The following morning when you came back from the bathroom and I'd put your hat on, and how you laughed and gave me that beautiful smile, you can't tell me that didn't mean anything to you even if

I have humiliated you, I hadn't done that then. I am not sorry for loving you whatever happens I always will. What frustrates me is you still don't understand why I did what I did. I guess I'm just going to have to live with that.

after I poured my heart out to him in the above message there was no reply. I sent numerous messages even tried to video call but there was never any response.

08/ 01/ 2022.

 **22:41**

I am really crazy about you Luca Oliveri forget sex we are so far away anyway, but the power of Facebook, means that no matter the distance between us, we can surely still be friends. Friendship can last a lifetime and is such a special bond between people, something so precious should not be cast aside without a second fault. Take care of yourself, you will always have a deep place in my heart.

I sent a gif two bearlike characters kissing with the words I love you so much, but they were still no reply. But then did I really expect one? Yes, always the eternal optimist.

09/ 01/ 2022

06:42.
Good morning.

Thank you, Luca.

 07:29.
You're welcome.

I was hoping the fact he said good morning to me, meant there was a slight thaw in his anger, I did not want to push it. So, I would leave him alone to get on with his day.

18:30.
Good evening.

 Goodnight.

I was starting to feel more confident, that although he was a long way off from forgiving me and probably never would, it did seem, but the anger was starting to subside. I really wish though that he would block me then all this heartache and hostility would be over between us. I kept telling myself, it was his arrogance that wouldn't allow him to do that, I was still boosting his ego. all this attention, my pathetic messages words of undying love for him it was probably the most attention he'd ever received in his life. The next day yet again in a moment of madness. I sent Luca one of his own photographs he was as I expected less than pleased but did not respond to the message Simply put an angry face to the right of his photograph, but I was not just going to accept it was over between us.

I really was hopelessly in love with this man, and I was going to fight to prove to him whatever the cost of my mental state, why would he just not accept that it was true.

 This is a man of my dreams, I love you. If you don't want me for God's sake, tell me!!!!!! Tell me Luca Oliveri, stop keeping me dangling on a string, just say it's over block me then this farce can come to an end once and for all. and you can eventually come to terms with the fact that I was a blight on your life and move on.

11/01/2022.
05:44.
Good morning my sexy shepherd, I love you.

Of course, I got the customary reply and that was it.

12/ 01/ 2022.

 19:44.

I'm in full mafia mode, you might want to take a look at my Facebook page, goodnight, Mr Oliveri.

 **Take my photo off your Facebook page. I did not give you permission to use my photo.**

In an attempt to get Luca to talk to me I had used one of my favourite photographs of him as my cover photo. It would be in a calculated risk, I knew he would reply, for it always being very protective of his privacy. I did notice right from the start the most modern photograph on his Facebook page dated back to 2015. This had always puzzled me, had something happened to him, or was he a mafioso but wanted to stay under the radar. My taking this call to action was bittersweet, he had replied, and at last he had done what I had been begging him for days to do. He had finally seen the light and had blocked me.

17/ 01/ 2022.

It had become a daily ritual to check messenger to see if I was still unable to contact Luca. So, imagine my surprise, that this morning I saw he had unblocked me.

 **10:38**

I don't understand why you unblocked me, but I am grateful.

This last week has been a nightmare, I have been so sad miserable, unable to sleep cried a lot, and being generally a pain in the arse around everyone else. I will send no nude photos, no hearts or kisses no romantic reflections. I will just talk to you like I do my other friends on Facebook. I know you are done with me in a romantic sexual context, I know you hate me, and I know deep in my heart you have every reason to feel like that. I hope you will find someone who loves you, as I wish I could have done. I have at last accepted, that in the end it was just sex for you, poor sex at that, but I hope we can sustain friendship if only on a casual basis after all my sheep binds us together. You never did ask me why I refer to them as my sheep or correct me and say no they are my sheep not yours.

 **I unblocked you for having a hard time with the other profile.**

I was at a loss to understand what he comments about the other profile unless he was returning back to the message sent to him by my friend Ernest. But he was a real person, it was not me pretending to be someone else, and although I had got Ernest to enhance the way I was feeling, it had in the main part being the truth. Of course, now he had unblocked me I couldn't help myself; I was desperate to prove to him how much I loved him.

 **18:26.**

Nice words and then you humiliated me by posting on my Facebook page the despicable things that you said that everyone could read. now you seem contrite, but it's

too late the damage was done when you posted on my Facebook page.

 **20:17**.

Oh, my dearest Luca I meant every word I ever said to you except for those horrible things which where uncalled for, I had too much wine and wanted to hurt you, but I've explained, and I did remove it as soon as I could. I'm amazed that you an intelligent man, can still not understand why I acted like I did, from my very first meeting you made me feel like $1,000,000, when I opened up my robe and you just said 'wow' I cannot put into words how you made me feel. I was sure that once you saw me full length naked, you would turn and run a mile. But you didn't you flung your arms around me and kissed me with such passion. No one has ever kissed me like that not even the mafioso Valerio. I know I didn't give you the one thing that would have really set the night on fire, but I was always brought up to believe that it was a sin, that God would not look favourably upon me if I took part in such an action, I've never wanted Salvatore, but you seem to believe he is my lover. He thinks I have Liggio's millions, we will always be friends, but we will never be lovers and that does not bother me, why? Because I had the good fortune to meet you, with every day that passes this stupid old love-struck woman love's you even more.

I continued to message, but the writing was on the wall, I think he'd only replied to let me know that he was still as he would say very angry with me, and that this time when he said he would never forgive me he had meant that from the bottom of his heart. Always a joke to Luca I had a dark Mafioso side, if it was true, I was Liggio's daughter I'd inherited some of his bad genes. but here I was again still the eternal optimist trying to convince myself that Luca was Just in one of his infamous moods.

21/ 01/ 2022.

It was dawn and I couldn't help myself.

 **04:53.**

Good morning, Mr. Oliveri, how are you?

08:46.
Good morning.

Thank you, Luca.

10:05.

Oh, Luca I'm trying so hard not to contact you, but this morning I broke down, because I had that wonderful dream last night. Ending on the sheepskin while you gently placed your beautiful cock up my arse. the passion extruding from you was magical as you thrust inside of me. I have never begged anyone for sex, but I know how much this meant to you so I'm willing to give you what you truly desire.

what do you want from me? Let me understand.

293

 **10:48.**

But you remember, how excited you were when I said I would do this one thing for you because I loved you so much.

There was no reply, so I decided to leave him alone and message later on in the day.

 **19:17.**

On the 14th of December, I said you shouldn't doubt yourself, you're awesome in bed would I have wanted to see you again if you were crap, I wanted to spend a whole week naked next to you.

I know my nose had just grown about three feet, but I had to try and massage his ego, or I was in danger of losing him forever. Not only was I being a liar, I was also being deceitful. I had no intention of letting him stick his penis anywhere near my backside, but he didn't need to know that.

 **19:50.**
Goodnight.

 21:01.

Thank you I will never give up on you. I really am crazy

about you honestly. G.

 22:30.

Oh, Luca, let me kiss you and caress your body just once more.

22/ 01/ 2021.

 03:37.

Good morning my sexy lover, have a good day I am really missing you.

 **05:05.**
Good morning.

20:41.

I had told him I would only say good morning and goodnight, so I had not messaged through the day, I just said goodnight to him now and it was reciprocated.

23/ 01/ 2022.

 **05:58.**
Good morning.

 **09:57.**

Good morning.

 **18:53.**
Since you said you love me so much [even if I don't believe you] help me realise my plans, so I can change my mind about you.

I replied I would do whatever he asked of me. Did he want me to move to Sicily, move in with him, even marry him? All he had to do was tell me. There was just silence, my message just went unread, there was no response until I suggested it was money he needed. With the covid pandemic I was sure it had been hard for so many businesses, maybe he as a sheep farmer had been through a hard time, not able to take sheep to market, had a profound effect on his finances, after all the sheep still needed to be fed, along with other livestock he may have, this suggestion really lit a fire under him and he responded with classic Luca anger as if somehow I had managed to insult him yet again.

 **Don't worry, I don't want money from anyone, but you just answered just as I imagined.**

I was furious this man's arrogance was starting to grate with me, I sent a vitriolic reply, then unsent the message. but it did prompt a reply from him, I was so annoyed that I had unsent the message because it meant I had no idea what I had said for him to respond. But it had obviously pricked his conscience because for the next few days we

296

exchanged good mornings good nights but nothing other than that then he suddenly sent a bizarre message.

 **I don't want anything in life, I have always done it alone.**
I just wanted confirmation and you gave it to me.

27 / 01 / 2022.

 **08:43.**
You only love yourself.

 No, Luca, I love you.

 **Have you not already proved it.**

Luca's messages were becoming more and more bizarre, once more I had no idea what it was that I was supposed to have already proved because I deleted a lot of my messages, a really stupid thing to do, I have not been able to go back and look at them, so they might have given me some idea what I was supposed to have proved? I sent another message to him which prompted an angry reply.

 **Then post on Facebook. It would not be the first time!!!!!**

 **11:19.**

I don't trust those who say they love me, much more those who stab me in the back. and you just happened to say you love me, and you stabbed me in the back.

This was more like the Luca of old, from what he was saying I could only assume he was relating back to the previous post; it would seem he was reiterating what he had said about never forgiving me, I also recalled him telling me that he could be someone's best friend or their worst enemy. I will soon discover how true that comment would prove to be in relation to me. I was going to be the one that was knifed in the back and in such a vitriolic spiteful way.

28/ 01/ 2022.

 **21:59.**

Oh no, I have just finished the last of my Don Corleone. I will take the bottle to bed and cuddle it, why? Because you bought it for me. I've also had a bottle of Sicilian wine so I'm a little happy, you will be very angry, I have downloaded the photo of you in your tractor, your shades on, cigar in your mouth. God, you look so sexy, then you always have been to me. I would like to fuck you in your tractor. I would rest my bum on the steering wheel, remove my panties and then sit on top of you, as you thrust into me. Every time you got into the tractor after that you would have that memory firmly fixed to the front of your mind. I miss you, your personality and that beautiful piece of equipment you have between your leg's goodnight my lover.

Luca just responded with a thumbs up to the right of the message, I had no idea what was going on in his head, it would seem he really did not give me a second thought but having said that he still seemed to be jealous towards Salvatore. It burned like a raging fire in his head, so I was not surprised by his next message, that came two days, after he said I had stabbed him in the back.

31/ 01/ 2022.

 **09:45**

Do you have sex with Salvatore?

I was furious with Luca, almost accused me of being a loose woman. I was sick of telling him there was nothing going on between Salvatore and I. He was a good friend, and I was very fond of his daughter nothing more than that. Although I was angry by his suggestion, I also felt a sense of elation, that Luca was still showing signs of jealousy. I mean after all why should he care less about who I might or might not be sleeping with, unless it was true that he did have feelings for me. But I was just deluding myself really, the more I thought about it I realised it was just his arrogance. How dare she sleep with another man when she says she loves me so much! I continued to message on a daily basis, but there was never any response no goodnight no good morning but as, yet I remained unblocked. Which led me to believe that he was not finished with me yet. Then I had one of those stupid ideas of mine, not putting the brain into gear before taking a course of action that was only going to make matters worse.

FEBRUARY
11/ 02/ 20 22.
09:55.

I sent a photograph of me naked in bed with an old flame, I knew it would arouse the jealous streak within Luca.

 Top guy knows what to do to please a woman, what was it you said unbridled passion this is what I had last night. Might not have been a Sicilian but God it was good. He wasn't just lying there like you did he has a cock to be proud of. He fingered me as I knelt down in the sheep position, just how you would have liked it Luca. God I was so vocal orgasm after orgasm, he licked me in fact he did all the things you just talked about. He was so excited I knew he had come because he too was vocal. When I made love with you, I didn't know if you ever came or not the only thing you did was disgusting and perverse. I did my best to boost yourself confidence, then it was all just bullshit Anyway. I did love you, but I will turn that love to hate, this guy is older than you, but he looks good for his age.

of course, once the message had been sent, I regretted my actions, and tried to remove it straight away, the problem was Luca must have been looking at his phone because he had read it before I got chance to delete.

10:45.

oh Luca, I am sorry.

 14:09.

I hated myself this morning, I cheated on you, because even now you still haven't blocked me, why not? Do you have feelings for me I'm sure you did in December; I don't care if you're not like Stan that was just sex. Because you left me so frustrated, I felt like a pressure cooker about to explode because the pressure could not escape. What we had wasn't just sex, what we shared was love I could never hate you. Even if you are mean to me, ignore me, don't talk to me. I still want you in my life.

 **I was certain you would let other men fuck you.**

 **15:00.**

wow Luca, a response. But you are wrong I don't sleep around not now never have ever. You fool I'm crazy about you, but you don't believe it's true, I am serious Luca you don't want me, do you? So why the hell should you care anyway. You've always said you don't believe a word I say, when I say I'm in love with you. Now you're trying to make out I have proved to you I am not to be trusted. It was a calculated risk sending the photo, saying I'd slept with this man. It was a ruse, a little white lie to see what your response would be, so I could glean some kind of understanding about your feelings. Oh yes, I was in bed with him naked, I can't really deny that when I've sent you the picture, but nothing happened between us. You and I had chemistry between us, a connection that has to count for something. you are the man in my head, in my heart, and the only man I want in my bed.

I sent numerous messages, but I never got a response.

23/ 02/ 2022.

I'll never forget it, it was a Wednesday, my friend Ernest came to my office, to find me sobbing at my desk. I always checked Luca's profile; I was not prepared for what I was about to see. his profile picture had always been a big tractor with a trailer and a smaller agricultural machine on the back of it. Today it had being replaced by a beautiful longhead blonde lady, with fishnet tights and knee length boots, she was lounging on the couch. Oh boy if he had wanted to make me jealous, he had certainly done that. I guess this was his way of telling me he had moved on only later that evening, he removed the picture and replaced it with his tractors, but I'd already downloaded it. Having spent the day glaring at it the little green monster within me became more and more intense. but I messaged him but as I expected there was no response. until I made the following threat.

 **20:28.**

I know how much you value your privacy, but I've decided to write a book about our doomed love affair, how the Godfather's daughter, seduced the quiet shepherd from

Corleone. It's not going to be a book of fiction; well how can it be when I'm going to use our messages to tell the story. I've been working on a flyer to publicise it when I come to Sicily in May. I'm going to display them around the town.

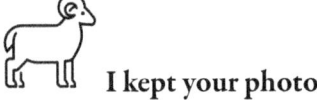 **I kept your photo.**

 So what Luca, I never told you I took photos of you while you slept in bed, in my bed Luca, at the hotel.

 Okay I have those of your naked breasts, the one of your vagina, and now this the one you sent me are you naked in bed, with who was it again Stan?

 **21:05**.

Well, I'm honoured, you get all excited when you look at my breasts. so, you kept them, but what can you do with them, apart from give me free publicity for my new book. Why are we fighting, you have nothing to do with me because you say I am a slut, that doesn't say much for you does it Luca, what the gifts, was that payment, sleep with many prostitutes do you?

25/ 02/ 22

 **09:46.**

Your girlfriend is very beautiful, I cannot compete with her.

303

I sent the picture of her to Luca.

 10:15.

meeting you was fate,

becoming your friend was a choice,

but falling in love with you, I had no control over.

Guilty.

 **But are you really convinced by doing so you will succeed in your intent.**

I was at a loss to understand, yet again one of his cryptic messages. I could only assume that it related to my having sent the photograph of his girlfriend. That had now disappeared, and a message was in its place saying that it had been removed because I did not have permission to share it.

I have never known such a ridiculous person.

He wasn't like this in December, when he kept coming to my bed, it would have been so easy once I got on the plane to just forget he had ever met me. But the romantic gestures, the phone call on Christmas Day, blowing all those kisses, appearing to be so glad to see me in person even if it was only over the Internet.

09:48.

Because I knew it would make him angry, I again changed my photograph to the one of him stood in front of his tractor.

 **So ridiculous.**

 Yes, it's ridiculous falling in love with a loser like you.

Believing you were an honest sincere man when all the time you're nothing more than a snake in the grass.

**You just made me laugh.
You are pathetic.**

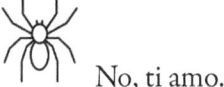 No, ti amo.

Siete sempre più patetici.

Boy I thought this man really knew how to twist the knife; did he really see me as pathetic had I just been a joke to him? Just gave him a chance to boost his arrogant Sicilian ego at my expense.

You can laugh at me, say that I am pathetic, well I wasn't pathetic was I when you came to my bed four times, came all the way to Palermo to fuck me, why bother!!!!! you bought me gifts, that to me meant a level of sincerity commitment or so I thought at the time, you're right though. I must be pathetic to care about an overweight bastard like you, the one who said you would never laugh at anyone, did not like teasing, not only arrogant but a hypocrite as well. Boy if you ask me, I've had a lucky escape. The one thing that I've never understood though, is why you seem so pissed off, not only that I might be having sex with Salvatore, that I might even drop my panties for some other man, when you have been fucking her for God knows how long. You're the one that's pathetic not me.

 10:33.

All this revenge because I said no to you sticking your cock up my arse, when you tried to do it anyway.

 Bastard.

Not as much as you.

The laughing emojis did not really bother me, it was the emojis of vomiting that upset me, was he really saying I made him want to be sick, then why keep coming and fucking me, he really was right when he said he could be someone's worst enemy, at the moment he was certainly mine.

Okay laugh but I will have the last laugh, I will be vindictive and spiteful, I will send a copy of the poster I will put up in Corleone when I have designed it, pathetic, yes as is your excuse for a cock, that everyone will know about. I was right about you when I wrote on your Facebook page about being as passionate as a corpse, she must have money if you are fucking her, stick it up her arse. I thought you liked big boobs. Hers are laughable, send your laughing emojis I will destroy you. this book will make you a laughingstock, tarnish your name being involved with the presumed daughter of a Mafia Godfather. as the saying goes Mr Luca arrogant Oliveri, 'The pen is mightier than the sword'.

 **You can do what you want, but you will never have me.**

This was war, I was going for the jugular, I was mystified why Luca had suddenly become so vitriolic, if he was so happy with a blonde bombshell why didn't he just block me, or did he have a twisted side to his nature. Was he getting some kind of perverse pleasure from being offensive and mean to me. The one man who had said once he could not abide people who made fun of others, he would never laugh at anyone So what was he doing to me right now?

 11;12.

I never had you in December with your pathetic excuse for a cock, so why should I care? I will find a man with a cock worth fucking. After all it's no loss to me, your excuse for a cock would probably have not got up my arse anyway. Vincenzo says you're not right in the head, goodbye Nutter, she will take all your money and dump you after all it can't be your pathetic cock she desires.

 **Good life Gigliola Liggio.**

That was it, it was over. he had blocked me; only this time, I hoped it was for good. I had this morning seen a side to this man, I had never seen before. Yes, there were times when he was angry, moody, but he'd never been nasty and vindictive like he had just been today. Yes, I would cry, mourn the loss, maybe in the end I would find more than just friendship with Salvatore but who knows at this moment in time certainly not I.